Her eyes roamed over hi **His black suit looked** **him. The white shirt tha** **the collar was sexy. He truly was one** **fine specimen of a man. There was no doubt as to why women swooned over him.**

"You want to get to know me better," Tamara said without preamble as she walked toward him. "Really get to know me?"

"Absolutely."

"Then how's this?" None too gracefully, she closed the distance between them. As she eased up on her toes, the thought that came into her mind was that she was definitely drunk with passion. She had no clue why she was doing what she was doing…nor could she stop herself.

Completely out of character, Tamara tipped up on her toes and planted her lips firmly on his. She gripped his shoulders for support. After about five seconds, she ended the kiss as quickly as she had initiated it.

Easing back, she looked up at Marshall and saw confusion on his face. She felt the same as her head swam.

Marshall's expression said that he was stunned…but also delighted. He raised an eyebrow. "Wow."

"That's what you wanted, isn't it?" she asked, her tongue feeling heavy. "To score?"

Books by Kayla Perrin

Kimani Romance

Island Fantasy
Freefall to Desire
Taste of Desire
Always in My Heart
Surrender My Heart
Heart to Heart
Until Now

KAYLA PERRIN

has been writing since the age of thirteen and once enter-
tained the idea of becoming a teacher. Instead, she has become a *USA TODAY* and *Essence* bestselling author of dozens
of mainstream and romance novels. She has been recognized
for her talent, including twice winning Romance Writers of
America's Top Ten Favorite Books of the Year Award. She has
also won the Career Achievement Award for multicultural
romance from *RT Book Reviews*. Kayla lives with her daugh-
ter in Ontario, Canada. Visit her at www.kaylaperrin.com.

Until Now

Kayla Perrin

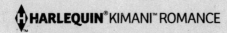

This book is dedicated to my readers who have endured the darker side of love. I hope you have come out on the other side stronger— knowing that you are worthy and beautiful and deserving of someone whose love lifts you up, not knocks you down.

Recycling programs
for this product may
not exist in your area.

ISBN-13: 978-0-373-86320-4

UNTIL NOW

Copyright © 2013 by Kayla Perrin

For questions and comments about the quality of this book, please contact us at CustomerService@Harlequin.com.

Printed in U.S.A.

HARLEQUIN®
www.Harlequin.com

Dear Reader,

If you read my Harts in Love series, then you'll recognize Tamara Jackson, who is the heroine of this novel. I'm happy to bring you back to Cleveland, Ohio, where you will see the Hart sisters again as you enjoy Tamara's story. You may remember that in *Always in My Heart,* Tamara was Callie's best friend who was trying to get out of an abusive marriage.

Sometimes, when love goes sour, it isn't just because people grow apart or because someone cheats. Sometimes, there is a more sinister reason.

I wanted to be able to explore a more serious element in this novel—dealing with the aftermath of domestic abuse—and show that healing is possible. More important, I wanted to show no matter the pain you have suffered, there is always hope for love.

I hope you enjoy the ride as Tamara and Marshall, also from *Always in My Heart,* overcome the obstacles in their lives in order to find lasting love.

As always, thank you for your continuing support!

Happy reading,

Kayla

Chapter 1

"You won't get away with this, you hear me? You think this is the end of it, but it's not over! I promise you that! *It's not over!*"

Patrick yelled at the top of his lungs, causing Tamara Jackson to flinch. Michael, her son, who was sitting beside her in the courtroom, gripped her hand tighter. With a sense of dread filling her belly, Tamara watched as her ex-husband was pulled toward the courtroom's exit. He was squirming, trying to free himself from the bailiffs' grip, and she was sure that if he could, he would lunge at her and cause her bodily harm.

"I'm gonna appeal, and I'll be out of here before you know it. And then you'd better be scared!"

The judge pounded her gavel. "Mr. Jackson, please calm down."

"He's not gonna get out, is he?" Michael asked.

Tamara looked down at her son's eyes that were wide with terror. "No, honey," she told him in a reassuring tone. "He's just trying to scare us because he's angry. He won't get out of jail for a very long time."

"I promise you—I'll be back!"

Bravely, Tamara watched Patrick being led out the door that would take him out of her view—and her life—forever. He twisted his head to give her one last glimpse and then he was gone.

A long, shuddery breath escaped Tamara. It was over. Patrick was gone. She never had to see him again.

"You okay?"

Tamara turned to face her mother, who was to her right. She instinctively loosened the grip on her hand. But Michael, on her left, was still holding tight to her other hand as if his life depended on it.

"I'm fine," Tamara said. She didn't feel fine right now, but she knew that she would be. Patrick was going to prison for forty-two years. He wouldn't be a problem again.

Though his promise still frightened her. She had spent years being afraid of him, and she couldn't simply turn off those feelings.

Tamara turned to her son, whose eyes were locked on the door Patrick had just exited through.

"Sweetheart, he's gone. He can't hurt us now."

"You promise?"

"Yes, I can promise you that." Tamara wrapped her arms around him and pulled him close. The prosecutor had assured her that there was no legal loophole for Patrick to file an appeal. The case against him had been ironclad.

Not only had Patrick threatened her and her son's lives, he had also tried to kill her best friend, Callie-Hart Williams—more than once. He'd been charged with kidnapping, two counts of attempted murder, assault causing bodily harm—a host of serious charges. Callie's testimony, earlier in the trial, had been moving and effective, and Tamara had seen a couple of the female jurors wiping away tears. The guilty verdict had been a foregone conclusion from the start.

"I love you," Tamara said, leaning over to rest her face atop Michael's head. "We have each other. We'll be all right."

"I love you, Ma," Michael said, his voice quavering.

Tamara's heart broke for him. No boy should have to sit in a courtroom like this and see his father sentenced to prison. But there was nothing she could do to change the events that had happened.

"Well, that's the end of that," Tamara's father commented and began to rise. "I never did like him."

Tamara bit her tongue. There was no point rehashing the fights she'd had with her parents in the past. No, they hadn't liked Patrick. But yes, she had married him nonetheless. The last thing she wanted to hear from her father now was I-told-you-sos. She had learned her lesson the hard way. All Tamara could do now was pick up the pieces of her life and move on.

And she was going to do so, literally. She was packed and ready to move back to Cleveland, where she had grown up. Callie had moved back there a year ago after Patrick had run her and her son, Kwame, off the road in an attempt to kill them both. As a result of returning to Cleveland, Callie had reconciled with her college sweetheart, who was also the father of the son he had never met. Now they were happily married. Callie and Nigel had invited Tamara and Michael to stay with them for as long as she wanted, and Tamara was taking them up on the offer.

Tamara kept her arms around her son as she stood, bringing him to his feet at the same time. One year. It had been one whole year since her world turned upside down. She was very much looking forward to putting the whole ugly ordeal behind her.

In a phone call, Callie had stressed to Tamara that she didn't need to be in the court to hear the sentencing. She had already been there to witness the verdict. And since Patrick had been found guilty on all charges, Callie assured her the sentence would be lengthy and there was no need to be in the courtroom to hear it. But Tamara knew the opposite to be true. She'd needed to be here. Needed to hear the sentence handed down. For her, it was all about closure.

In the time since Patrick's arrest, Tamara had gone through

a year of counseling to deal with everything, not only for herself but also for her son. The counseling sessions had helped her understand what had drawn her to a man like Patrick in the first place.

The most important thing she had come away with was that she had to forgive herself. Sometimes, all you could do was learn from your mistakes, and this was one of those times. Tamara was wiser now in terms of knowing the signs to look for when it came to dangerous men. And she understood what had led her to make some of the decisions she had. Why she had chosen Patrick, why she had stayed. But in the end, the ownership of the behavior belonged to Patrick. She could not blame herself for what he had done.

Part of what she had learned in therapy was that she had been drawn to men who needed nurturing. It was amazing how you could think you had your life together, how you could see other people's problems, and yet so dismally fail at recognizing your own. Tamara had never put together the pieces that having had a father who was emotionally distant had led her to pick men who were like injured birds. Men she believed that with her love she could help learn to fly again.

"I do wish you would reconsider moving to Cleveland," her mother said once they were out of the courtroom.

"I know," Tamara said. She had already heard their objections to her plan. "But it's something I have to do." Tamara's parents believed the move would be temporary. But Tamara had other plans. She had taken a leave of absence from her job just in case, but she had every intention of making Cleveland her home again.

A new but familiar start…

"Right now you need to be with your family," her mother stressed. "We want to help you through this."

"And you have. In this past year, you've helped me a lot. I understand that you're worried, but Michael and I will be okay. Being here in Florida…emotionally, I can't handle it. And Michael has had a tough time, too. I think it's best for both of us that we put Florida behind us, at least for the time being."

"You're leaving your job behind," her father piped in. "How do you intend to survive?"

"I have savings," Tamara said. "And I can get another job. I can work in real estate in Cleveland if I have to."

Her father scoffed, and Tamara tried to ignore the wave of disappointment washing over. She was thirty-two, a mother and entitled to make her own decisions. She didn't need her parents' approval.

Now, of all times in her life, she needed to stand on her own two feet. But she didn't dare mention her future plans to her parents at this point—which included a change in career paths—because they would surely object.

"I know you'll miss me," Tamara said gently. "I'll miss you, too. But I'm going to be with Callie and Nigel, and Michael will have his old friend Kwame to make the transition easier. Please understand, this is something I need to do."

A look of resignation passed over her mother's face, and then she pulled Tamara into an embrace. "I love you. Your father and I just want the best for you."

"I know that."

"You're heading out tomorrow, then?" her father asked, and Tamara could tell that he was holding in his emotions. He had been emotionally aloof all of his life, but she knew that he loved her.

"Yes," she answered. "In the morning, we'll start the drive."

"You are still coming for dinner?" her mother asked hopefully.

"Yes." Tamara smiled. "Yes, of course."

Tamara looked at Michael, who had been silent during the conversation. His eyes were downcast, and she could only imagine what he was thinking.

Her poor son. Eight years old now, and he had endured more than he should. He deserved a father who loved him, not one who had made their household a nightmare. Things had soured for Patrick when he'd lost his high-paying consultant job and couldn't find a new position. He'd turned to the bottle and spiraled out of control. On more than one occasion, he'd belabored the point that he was the man, and that he should be able to provide for his family. No matter how many times Tamara had reminded Patrick that they were still doing well, that they hadn't lost everything, that their savings were going to see them through until he got another job, he didn't want to hear it.

Stop thinking about Patrick, she told herself. She knew it was easier said than done. But with her divorce decree in hand as of last week, and Patrick's sentencing today, things were already looking better.

"You know," her father began, "there's no reason that you have to leave so soon. Your house hasn't even sold yet."

"Callie's sister is getting married on Saturday," Tamara said, something she had already explained.

"I understand that," her father said. "But you can fly out there for a few days, enjoy the wedding and then come back. I don't understand why you're selling your house if it's a temporary move."

"Because she doesn't want to live in the house she shared with Patrick," her mother pointed out, sounding a little exasperated. "Surely you can understand that, Howard."

"Yes, that makes sense," he said. "But shouldn't she be here to see about securing another property, at—"

"I want to go to Cleveland," Michael suddenly interjected.

Surprised, Tamara and her parents all looked down at him.

"Tomorrow," Michael went on, looking at Tamara, his eyes pleading. "I don't want to wait."

"I know, baby." Tamara stroked his face, feeling his pain. She knew it hadn't been easy for her son in the months after his father's arrest. The kids at school hadn't been kind. They'd had to stay in Florida to deal with the charges and the trial, but it was clear now that Michael was ready for a fresh start as much as she was.

She placed her hands on his shoulders and looked him in

the eye. "Don't you worry, son. We're going to Cleveland to-morrow, just as planned."

Cleveland represented a new beginning.

A new life.

Chapter 2

A trial, a divorce and a wedding.

Tamara played the words over in her mind as she drove into Cleveland, thinking that she might just have come up with the next winning title for a British comedy. Starring Idris Elba, of course—one seriously fine British brother.

Only Idris wouldn't play her crazed ex-husband. No, he would have to be a new, sexy stranger who would come into her life.

Tamara rolled her eyes and chuckled mirthlessly, then concentrated on the task at hand—looking for the exit that would lead her to St. John African Methodist Episcopal Church. Why were her thoughts even heading in the direction of any type of sexy stranger? Now that her divorce was final, she was literally and figuratively free of anyone holding her back, and the last thing she was interested in was dating. Her only focus was herself and her son completely.

A short while later, Tamara exited Interstate 490 and headed onto East Fifty-Fifth Street. She maneuvered her way to Cedar Avenue, where the historic church was located. As she reached the church, she saw a white Bentley parked outside the front. A bow adorned the car's front emblem, with two lengths of white ribbon extending to the side mirrors. White ribbon was also looped through the wrought-iron railings lining the steps, and capped off with bows at the top and bottom. A red carpet extended from the church doors down the steps to the road where the car was parked.

It was elegant and beautiful. And reminded Tamara of her own wedding day. She inhaled sharply with the memory. She didn't want to think about that day, not with the reality of how horribly her marriage had turned out.

Tamara turned into the parking lot and found an available space without too much trouble. She spent a few minutes touching up her makeup, which was all the time she could afford. She was running a little later than she had hoped, getting to the church with about twelve minutes to spare before the ceremony was to begin. She'd taken an extra day during her drive from Florida, which meant she had to travel on the day of Deanna's wedding, and that had put her a bit behind schedule.

"You ready, Michael?" Tamara said as she opened the back door for her son.

He nodded, but his eyes were still glued to his Nintendo DS gaming system.

"Okay. Time to put away your DS. We have to go inside and get a seat."

Tamara wished she had gotten to Cleveland earlier so that she could have changed into her dress at Callie's house. But traveling with Michael, she hadn't wanted to spend two excessively long days on the road. So driving this morning had been a must. As Michael got out of the car, she smoothed the back of her dress, hoping that the three-hour car ride hadn't made it too wrinkled. Then she grabbed the blazer for Michael's suit from the backseat and helped him into it.

Tamara hurried into the church with Michael. An usher handed her a glossy wedding program, with a lovely photo of Deanna and Eric posing on either side of a tree. Then Tamara

and Michael headed into the sanctuary and settled in seats
halfway up on the bride's side.

"Where's Kwame?" Michael asked.

"I don't know, son, but he might be in the wedding. You'll
see him later."

Michael nodded but didn't look up. His gaze was on his
hands. Tamara put her arm around him and squeezed. A year
had passed since Michael had seen Kwame, and Tamara had no
doubt that the boys would pick up where they'd left off. There
was a two-year age difference between them, and Kwame had
always been like a big brother to Michael.

Kwame's relationship with Michael was one of the reasons
that Tamara made the decision to head back to Cleveland. She'd
grown up here, but left for Florida when her parents moved
there. Later, she'd started college there, and Callie had come
down to join her in the "sunshine state" after she got pregnant.

Tamara looked around, taking in the various guests at the
church. Through the windows in the doors at the back of the
church, she caught a glimpse of Callie moving around. She
smiled, as she always did when she saw her friend. Then she
glanced at the clock hanging above the doors. Two minutes
until noon. Looked as though this wedding was going to start
on time.

Tamara looked over her shoulder again and saw a man and
woman briskly entering the church just as a man was prop-
ping the back doors open. The woman was striking, wearing
a red dress that was cut too low for the occasion and looked as
if it could have been painted on. The man had his hand on the
small of the woman's back as they walked forward and quickly
slipped into a pew closer to the front.

As the smiling man glanced backward, Tamara drew in a
sharp breath. She recognized the handsome face.

Oh, my goodness, it was Marshall Jennings. She hadn't seen
him in thirteen years, but certainly could never forget him.
Tall, fit and seriously fine, he'd been known as a playboy. A
rich playboy who'd had his share of the women in Cleveland.

Tamara's cousin, Gloria, had been one of those women. At first, Gloria had been thrilled with the attention Marshall had doled on her. But in the end, she had been devastated when he had quickly moved on to a new woman after getting her into his bed.

Tamara remembered that Marshall had been a friend of Nigel's, and perhaps she would have seen him at Callie and Nigel's wedding months ago—if she had been able to attend. But a winter storm had ravaged the eastern seaboard, canceling flights all over the country. Hers had been one of them, and she'd been crushed that she hadn't been able to make it to Cleveland for her best friend's winter wedding. That was why—even if she had to drive forty-eight hours straight—she would not have missed Deanna's special day.

Tamara noticed the woman in red lean close and whisper into Marshall's ear. Could she be his wife?

The classical music that had been playing in the church stopped, and the opening score of an instrumental love ballad began. The groom and his groomsmen entered from a door near the rostrum and took their place on the right side. It would have been easy to spot Eric even if Tamara hadn't seen his picture on the program. He was the one beaming from ear to ear.

Once the men were in place, two flower girls started down the aisle. The crowd oohed and aahed at the darling little girls. Tamara realized that she was right—Kwame was in the wedding—when she saw him carrying the rings down the aisle on a pillow made of white satin. Then came the bridesmaids, followed by Callie, the matron of honor. Tamara looked at her friend and grinned. Callie spotted her and her eyes brightened as she smiled back at her.

A woman walked onto the rostrum, and a few moments later, the music changed again. A man at a piano at the front of the church began to play something soft and romantic. Then the woman began to sing. Everyone stood and looked toward the back of the church, where the bride now stood with her arm looped through her uncle's.

And then the bridal march began. Deanna looked beautiful in an off-the-shoulder dress made of satin. It was a closely fitted gown that flared at the bottom. As Deanna passed her, Tamara could see that her eyes were filled with happy tears.

Once Deanna was at the front of the church, Tamara's eyes went back to Marshall. With his hand on his guest's back, she could see now that he wasn't wearing a wedding ring.

So the woman wasn't his wife. If Tamara had to bet, she would guess that the woman was just a plaything he had picked up so he could have her on his arm for this occasion. The Marshall she had known had liked flashy cars and flashy women. And this woman certainly fit that bill.

Eric took his bride by the hands. The minister stood before them with a large smile, and then the ceremony began.

And despite the fact that Tamara was freshly divorced, she got caught up in the magic of the day.

Tamara didn't have the chance to say more than a few words to Deanna until the reception, once the meals were consumed and the dancing began. She was sitting at a table with Deanna's mother and uncle and some of the extended family members. Michael had gone home with Kwame, where a babysitter was watching them now. At least at the table with family, Tamara didn't feel awkward for not having a date.

Spotting Deanna speaking with a couple of young females at the edge of the dance floor, Tamara rose from the table and started toward her. Seeing her approach, Deanna's eyes lit up, and she stretched open her arms in the offer of a hug.

"Tamara," Deanna said in a singsong voice as Tamara walked into her embrace. "I'm so glad you could make it."

"Of course," Tamara told her. As she pulled back, she took Deanna's hands in hers and squeezed. "Congratulations, Dee. I'm so happy for you and Eric. He seems like a great guy."

"Thank you." Deanna's smile was as bright as the sun. "He is a great guy. An old friend I never saw as anything more than a friend until I came back to Cleveland and we got to know each other."

"You both look very happy."

"We are. And I can hardly believe it. When I came back to Cleveland, I never thought that I would find love. In fact, that was the last thing on my mind. Yet, here I am. Married."

"Let me see the ring." Deanna extended her left hand, and Tamara eyed the stunning engagement ring and wedding band encrusted with diamonds around the entire band. "Gorgeous."

"Thank you. Of course, it's not about the ring. It's about the man." Her eyes lit up as she glanced beyond Tamara's shoulder. "And there's my baby now."

Deanna looked up at her new husband with a loving smile, and he grinned down at her as he came beside her and slipped an arm around her waist. It was a beautiful moment between two people who loved each other, and reminded Tamara that relationships were fundamentally good. She had just been with the wrong man.

Tamara extended her hand to Eric. "Eric, it's a pleasure to meet you. I'm Tamara, Callie's best friend."

"Ah, yes. I've heard a lot about you. Nice to meet you, and thank you for coming."

"Thank you for having me. Your ceremony was beautiful, and the reception has been exceptional."

"Thank you," Eric said.

"Where are you two heading for your honeymoon?" Tamara asked.

They both looked at each other, as if determining who would answer. A moment later, Deanna spoke. "Well, we wanted to do something different than the typical Caribbean honeymoon. Eric has always wanted to go to Scotland, so that's where we're headed. We're going for two weeks to tour the country. We'll even be staying in an old castle and everything."

Eric pulled Deanna close. "I'm not the type of guy who likes to just sit on the beach for seven days. When I want rest and relaxation, I go to my parents' cottage on the lake. I wanted our honeymoon to be an adventure."

"It will be. As long as we're together." Deanna looked like the happiest woman alive. "As long as I'm with you, I don't care where we go."

"Well, congratulations again. You both look very happy, and that's what matters."

Tamara was walking away when suddenly she felt a hand on her arm. She turned to see that it was Deanna who had touched her. Deanna walked a few more steps with her, out of earshot of Eric, and asked, "How did everything go in Florida?"

Tamara made a face as she shrugged. "As well as can be expected. Patrick got what he deserved—a forty-two-year prison sentence. And I got my closure. But it was emotionally draining for me and for Michael. Of course, Patrick was livid. He uttered more threats as he was dragged out of the courtroom, saying that he'll get out on appeal and then I'll be sorry." Tamara waved a dismissive hand. "But I'm not afraid of him."

"Good," Deanna told her. "With what he did, there's no way he's going to get out of prison. He can't hurt you any more. And if he ever does live to see freedom, he'll be old and certainly won't be dumb enough to try to come after you."

"I know. I'm not worried about him."

"That's good," Deanna told her. "I just wanted to add that I know you might be feeling out of sorts and uneasy, but we're all here for you. I went through my own scare with a crazy ex—nothing as serious as your situation, of course—but still, there's life after an abusive relationship." Now Deanna smiled. "For me, coming back to Cleveland was what led to my ultimate happiness."

"Are you trying to forecast that I'm going to find love here, too?" Tamara asked, flashing Deanna a look of mock skepticism.

"It's my wedding day. I guess it's fair to say I'm full of hopeful optimism."

Behind Deanna, Tamara noticed Marshall enter the banquet

hall. He'd eaten dinner, then left, and Tamara had thought he wasn't coming back.

Not that she was keeping tabs on him.

"Basically, I just wanted to make sure that you were okay," Deanna continued.

"I'm good. Actually, I'm happy to be back here. Over the last year, I've gone through a lot of counseling. Both me and Michael. I feel strong. And I'm ready to make changes in my life for the better."

"Good."

The song changed from an upbeat tune to a slow ballad, and Deanna instantly turned. "I should get back to my groom."

"Of course."

Tamara watched Deanna hurry back to Eric, remembering how happy she had been on her own wedding day. How in love. How she had wholeheartedly believed her marriage to Patrick would last forever.

Stop thinking about Patrick, she told herself. *This is Deanna and Eric's day, and they're going to have a wonderful life together.* Tamara was certain of that. Just looking at them, she knew they had that inexplicable X factor she and Patrick hadn't. The ease of communication, the obvious respect. A gentle kind of love that would carry them through the hard times.

"Can I have this dance?"

Tamara turned. And her heart slammed against her rib cage when she saw Marshall standing there.

"Excuse me?" she said.

"May I have this dance?" Marshall repeated and extended a hand to her.

Well, this was a surprise. He hadn't given her more than a fleeting glance after the ceremony, and he had passed her by when everyone had been mingling at the reception hall. She had, however, caught his eye more than once, but the fact that he hadn't made a point of saying hello had led her to believe that he wasn't interested in talking to her.

And now here he was, asking for a dance.

"You want to dance with me?" Tamara asked.

"Why do you seem so surprised? A beautiful woman like you? What man in his right mind wouldn't?"

Tamara narrowed her eyes. Didn't he remember her? All this time, she had expected him to approach her to say hello. When he hadn't, she'd assumed it was because of his date. Some women got irrationally jealous if their man talked to another female. But now, as he looked down at her, Tamara figured that he must not remember her. Surely if he knew who she was, he would address her with a sense of familiarity.

"Don't make me beg," Marshall continued, the corners of his lips lifting in a charming smile. "This is a wedding. I assure you, I'm not some creep from off the street."

That confirmed it. He had no idea who she was. It was a little bit humorous, in fact. He had gone after her cousin with such steadfast determination that he had obviously taken no note of her.

"All right." Tamara took his proffered hand, smirking with the secret knowledge that he was clueless.

Marshall led her the short distance to the dance floor and then took her in his arms and pulled her close. Her breasts flattened against the hard wall of his chest, and the unexpected sensation of his body against hers caused her breathing to halt for a few seconds.

What a physique he had. His chest was muscular and strong, and so were his shoulders where she'd brought her hands to rest. She hadn't been able to see his sculpted figure beneath his suit, but she could certainly feel how fit he was now that they were dancing.

Of course he had a magnificent body. A man like Marshall would make sure to stay in tip-top shape for the ladies.

He pulled her a little closer and lowered his hand down her back, causing a shiver to dance down her spine. His hand stayed a respectable distance above her behind, but the warmth of it emanated through her dress and across her skin. And when his fingertips urged her even closer, she felt a startling flush.

It had to be the wine, she told herself. She'd had a couple of glasses with dinner. Clearly, the alcohol was getting to her head.

"See? No reason to fear me," he said into her ear, his voice low and deep.

And as if he had whispered sweet nothings in her ear, she felt another flush.

Okay, so maybe it wasn't the wine. Maybe it was the fact that Marshall was a manly man, one who knew how to touch a woman, how to look at her and make her feel incredibly beautiful. That was all a part of his charm, and clearly Tamara wasn't immune to it. And that surprised her.

Though maybe she shouldn't be surprised. Obviously, she wasn't dead. A woman would have to be blind and without any senses at all to not know that Marshall was an attractive man. More than attractive. He was *fine.*

And not only did he look good and feel good, he smelled good.

Tamara's eyes widened with alarm. Why on earth was she thinking about the fact that he smelled good?

"I hear you're from Cleveland," he said, distracting her from her thoughts. "How is it I've never seen you around before?"

"You've seen everyone within the city limits?" Tamara challenged.

He eased back to look down at her. "Someone like you I would have noticed."

Tamara leaned her head forward so that he wouldn't see her face and rolled her eyes. He was so predictable. Did every player in the world have to comment on how odd it was that an attractive woman had escaped his prowl?

"I didn't exactly look like this when I moved from Cleveland the summer after my freshman year of college. I was too skinny, had no fashion sense. I didn't attract a lot of male attention."

"I find that very hard to believe."

Tamara eyed him, thinking it ironic that he didn't realize his very words were proving her point. Obviously, her very boring appearance had to be why he hadn't noticed her when he was dating Gloria. True, she hadn't met him many times, but it was clear that his encounters with the shy, gawky kid she'd been had not been memorable.

One of the reasons Tamara had been drawn to Patrick when they'd met was because he had seemed smitten with her. Patrick had been older, worldly, and saw her as a diamond in the rough in a sea of more sophisticated women. Ironic, when Tamara had started to become a more confident person, Patrick hadn't liked it.

"I didn't hang out much," Tamara added. "I was more of a bookworm. I didn't do the club scene."

"Maybe that explains it," Marshall said. "You must have been hidden away somewhere. Your father was probably afraid to let you out into the world."

Tamara rolled her eyes again. So he really had no clue.

A few seconds later, when the song ended, Tamara began to ease back. "Well, thanks for the—"

"Oh, no no no. I'm not ready to let you go yet. The music is still slow. We can keep dancing."

She eyed him with curiosity as the Charlie Wilson song began to play. "Seriously, don't you think your date will get upset?" Tamara hadn't seen the woman in a while, but she didn't have to see her to know that a second dance with another woman would no doubt irk his date.

"My date?" Marshall looked confused. "Oh, my cousin. She left."

"Your cousin?" Tamara asked doubtfully.

"So you noticed me," Marshall said, sounding amused.

"Who wouldn't?" Tamara countered. "Tell me, was her dress painted on?"

Marshall chuckled, a throaty sound that was all too enticing. "Renee likes attention, I'll give you that. She had to head home right after dinner. She agreed to accompany me because I didn't have a date."

Now Tamara was the one who laughed. "You don't strike me as the kind of man who has a hard time finding a date. Unless, of course, you've gone through all the women in Cleveland…"

"Ah!" Marshall exclaimed, his lips widening in a grin. "I like you. You're funny."

She wasn't trying to be funny. She was diplomatically letting him know that she knew exactly what kind of man he was.

But the interchange between them was becoming more interesting by the second, and she was suddenly feeling a little mischievous.

"So, what's your name?" she asked, her voice taking on a little flirtatious subtext.

"Marshall," he answered. "And I've already heard your name. Tamara."

"That means you've inquired about me?"

"Like I said, I noticed you. And I understand that you're back in town for a while."

"You've certainly done your homework." Tamara looked up at him and gave him a quizzical look, and even batted her eyelashes. She would play his game. Play it so she could get the satisfaction of rejecting him.

"Someone like you—of course I did my homework."

"My, is this how you are with all the women? Total silver tongue?"

"You've got me all wrong," Marshall said. "If you're implying that I'm simply a sweet-talker, that's not me."

Again, Tamara eased back to look at him. "You're telling me that you haven't broken your fair share of hearts?"

"I've had my heart broken, too."

Yeah right, Tamara thought. Men like Marshall didn't get their hearts broken, because they didn't have a heart. When it came to relationships, all that mattered were the notches on their bedposts. Men like Marshall stayed with a girl until he grew bored with her. Then quickly moved on.

His hand went to her upper back and urged her closer. Tamara's cheek pressed against pecs that were rounded with muscles. And—she couldn't help noting—a perfect place for a woman to lay her head.

Good grief, what was wrong with her?

The second song ended, and Tamara slid her hands down Marshall's arms and began to step backward. "Again, thank you for the dance," Tamara said, pulling her bottom lip between her teeth.

She saw Marshall's eyes widen with lust, and she had to inwardly smile. Yeah, she had his number. All a woman had to do was bat her eyelashes and give him a little bit of feminine charm, and he would eat it up.

"You're leaving me already?" Marshall asked once she had maneuvered herself out of his arms.

"Fast song. And I have two left feet." She smiled sweetly.

He came to stand beside her and leaned into her. "Let's go to my table, then...to talk."

"Thank you," Tamara reiterated firmly. "The dance was nice."

"But I haven't even begun to get to know you."

Tamara simply shrugged, then started to walk away.

Marshall fell into step beside her. "I see. You're going to make me chase you."

"Aren't there some other attractive women here that you'd like to get to know?"

"The only woman I'm interested in getting to know here is you. Trust me on that."

Tamara already knew his game. He liked a challenge. He had chased Gloria until she finally gave in, and once she had surrendered to him, that had been it. The thrill for Marshall had been gone.

"I'll see you around, Marshall."

"Oh, no, you don't."

But when Marshall placed a hand on her arm, Tamara shrugged out of his touch and kept walking. Seconds later, she turned to look over her shoulder and saw him standing and staring after her with his hands placed on his hips and his bottom lip pulled between his teeth.

Poor Marshall. He clearly had no clue how to handle rejection.

Tamara chuckled as she made her way over to Callie.

Chapter 3

"Tamara," Marshall said as he pulled out a chair and took a seat beside Nigel. "I want to know everything about her."

Nigel looked at him askance. "Didn't I just see you dancing with her?"

"Yes. But it ended too soon."

"Ahh, rejected," Nigel said with a grin.

"Feels more like a game to me," Marshall said. Tamara had undoubtedly flirted with him. And now she wanted to see if he would chase her. "Tell me about her."

"She's been Callie's friend for years. She's the one who Callie had to go to Florida to testify for."

"Ahh, that's right. The one with the crazy ex."

"So I wouldn't say she's playing any cat-and-mouse games. I seriously doubt she's ready for any of that." Nigel looked him dead in the eye. "You're interested?"

"Can you blame me?" Marshall looked in her direction. "Look at her. She's gorgeous."

"And she's off-limits," Nigel said.

Marshall jerked his gaze back to Nigel, frowning. "She just

ended her marriage. You telling me she's already dating someone else?"

"No, I mean she's off-limits to *you*."

Marshall began to smile. "Should I be offended?"

"What I'm trying to say is that she's had a rough year. She's
just closed the door on her abusive ex-husband. She's not the
typical girl you like to hook up with, the kind who's interested
in having a hot fling and nothing more."

Marshall nodded. "So basically you're telling me I should
stay away from her because you think I'd hurt her."

"Not on purpose. But considering I doubt she wants what
you want, yeah, I see the risk of her getting hurt."

"No worries, Nigel. I'm not planning to hurt her. I'd just
like to get to know her a little bit better."

Nigel gave him a knowing look.

"You telling me I can't even talk to her?"

"You're a big boy. I'd never tell you that. But she is Callie's
friend, which means I want to look out for her. She's got to be
vulnerable right now, so I would take that into consideration."

"I'm your best friend, Nigel. You know I'm not some evil guy."

"Of course not. If you were, we wouldn't be friends. Just...
keep in mind what I said. She's fresh out of her marriage, so I
don't imagine she'd be interested in anything. But I do know
that I don't want to see her hurt any further."

"Duly noted."

Marshall looked in her direction again and caught her looking at him. She quickly averted her eyes. He smiled, because
he'd caught her looking.

Oh, yeah, she was interested in him. At the very least, she
liked what she saw. She hadn't told him to get lost, and then
there had been that whole flirtatious exchange. Marshall knew
when a woman found him attractive.

But she was vulnerable. He could deal with the fact that
she'd been hurt.

Because he wasn't planning to cause her any more pain.

In fact, his thoughts were far from that.

* * *

Half an hour later, the crowd was cheering as Eric made a production of taking the garter belt off of his bride's thigh. With Deanna seated in a chair, Eric teased her as he slipped his hands beneath her gown, much to the crowd's delight, and lowered the blue garter. As people whistled and clapped, he gripped the garter with his teeth once it was past her knee and dragged it down to her ankle.

The crowd went wild.

Deanna blushed as Eric finally pulled the garter over her toes. Then he jumped to his feet, triumphant.

"All the single men, get ready for the garter toss," the DJ announced.

The eligible men went to the dance floor behind Eric and vied for the best position to catch the garter. Tamara and the guests laughed as Eric pretended he was going to throw it one way—more than once—before ultimately tossing it over his shoulder high to his far right.

Marshall, who'd actually been standing just left of Eric about ten feet back, leaped so far to the right that he was able to snag the material with the tips of his fingers. Victorious, he secured it in his fist and did a little dance while the other men around him accepted defeat.

"Of course," Tamara muttered.

"What was that?" Callie asked her.

"Nothing."

"And now it's time for the single ladies. All single ladies to the dance floor for the bouquet toss!"

When Tamara didn't move, Callie made a face at her. "Aren't you getting up?"

Tamara scoffed. "I don't think so."

"Come on, Tamara. It'll be fun."

Tamara shook her head. "There are plenty of single ladies getting up already."

"Most of whom look too young to get married. Get your butt up there."

"It's not nec—"

"Last call for all the single ladies to the dance floor," the DJ said. "Don't be shy."

"You heard him." Callie got up from her chair and approached Tamara.

"What are you doing?" Tamara protested as Callie reached for her hand.

"Just get up. Come on. This is the fun part."

With Callie physically taking her hand, Tamara sighed and stood. Those around her cheered as she made her way to the dance floor.

As if she wanted to catch the bouquet after Marshall had caught the garter.

Fine. I can stand here, but I don't have to be the one to catch the cursed thing. While some of the teenagers around her looked supereager, Tamara resisted the urge to roll her eyes.

Then the music began, and as Eric had done, Deanna teased the teen girls and adult women by pretending she was about to release the bouquet. And then she did.

And it sailed in the air straight toward Tamara.

Reflexively—so the bouquet didn't hit her in the face— Tamara caught it. And then people began to cheer, and she realized what she had done.

But the realization truly hit her when she looked to the edge of the dance floor and saw Marshall standing there, grinning at her as if he had just won the lottery.

"Give them a round of applause, ladies and gentlemen," the DJ said with enthusiasm. People clapped. "And welcome the couple to the dance floor to share a dance!"

The guests cheered and whistled their encouragement for Tamara and Marshall to dance. And then Marshall began to approach her.

Tamara's stomach sank. Good Lord, would she never escape the man?

"So we meet again," Marshall said as he stopped before her. "How fitting."

Tamara swallowed. What she wanted to do was flee. But with all of the wedding guests watching with smiles on their faces, that was the last thing she could do.

The DJ began to play Eric Benét's "I Wanna Be Loved," and there was nothing Tamara could do but accept her fate when Marshall slipped his hands around her waist and pulled her close.

Her stomach fluttered, and her body tensed.

"That's right," the DJ said, urging them on, "get to know each other."

All eyes were on them as if the guests believed that Cleveland's newest couple had just been crowned.

"Smile," Marshall told her. "People are going to start wondering what's wrong."

Tamara inhaled a shaky breath and then tried her best to force a smile. She had enjoyed the dancing when it had been on her terms, but now it was as if fate was laughing at her.

"You're as stiff as a board," Marshall whispered. "What happened to the woman I was dancing with earlier tonight?"

That woman had been playing a game, or so she'd thought.

"I'm not exactly comfortable with public attention," Tamara said by way of explanation.

"It's just a dance. Not a date with the executioner."

Tamara wished that his voice wasn't so deep and sultry. And that he wouldn't whisper into her ear the way he did, as if they had developed some sort of comfort level already.

She tried to ease back as far as possible without looking uncomfortable, and when the song came to an end, she was relieved. It was clear to her that she'd lit Marshall's fire, so to speak, and that he was interested.

"Excuse me," she said and stepped away from him.

"Where are you going?" he asked.

"I need a drink," she told him. She felt as if her whole body was burning up.

"I'll join you."

Tamara headed toward the punch table. She had abstained from the cocktail when she'd arrived at the reception, but with Marshall on her heels, she poured a full cup and gulped it down.

She saw Marshall looking at her with humor in his eyes as he slowly poured a cup and sipped the beverage. Humor and determination.

"Now, if you'll excuse me." Tamara put her empty cup on the edge of the table and plastered a smile on her face. "Nature calls."

"Excellent," Marshall said. He started for the doors with her. "We'll go together."

Tamara's eyes widened in horror. "What?"

Marshall placed a hand on her upper back and kept walking with her.

"W-what are you doing?" Tamara asked, looking over her shoulder at him in disbelief.

"Not what you think I'm doing." With one hand, Marshall pushed open one of the double doors, and with the other, he whisked her out of the ballroom. "I just want to talk."

Tamara expelled a frustrated breath. "You're following me because you want to *talk?*"

"You're having fun with this, aren't you?" Marshall countered, coming to a stop several feet away from the reception-hall doors.

"Because I have to go to the bathroom?"

"You dance with me, leave me thinking you're interested, and now you seem as though you can't get away from me fast enough."

Tamara stared up at him…and her vision momentarily blurred. She felt a little odd. A bit dizzy. But she forged ahead. "I need to go to the bathroom, and you take that as rejection?"

"You know what I'm talking about," Marshall countered, his full lips twisting. "I just want to know—what happened to the woman on the dance floor earlier? The one who made it clear she wanted me to chase her?"

Tamara guffawed. "Chase me?"

"I bet you're planning to leave here and not give me a way to reach you. And tonight in your bed, you'll have a laugh at my expense, right?"

"You know you sound crazy."

"And you called *me* the heartbreaker," he went on, shaking his head while his eyes danced with humor.

Amazing, Marshall didn't seem perturbed by anything. He had the carefree manner of a man who had it easy in life.

"I'm sorry if you think—"

"Here's the interesting thing, Tamara. Nigel's my best friend. We work together. So whether or not you give me your number, I'll be seeing you again. So why don't we get past this game part—as fun as it is—and just exchange numbers now."

"My, my, my. You certainly have a way with women, don't you?"

Marshall threw his head back and laughed. "Am I coming off too strong? Sorry. It's just…" His eyes roamed over her face. "Damn, I'm not sure what it is. All I know is that I'm interested."

"What exactly are you interested in?"

"In getting to know you better."

Tamara felt a little woozy again and knew she needed to splash some cold water over her face. "Can we please continue this conversation when I come out of the bathroom?"

"Sorry. Of course."

Tamara found the door to the restroom a few steps away. Before she went inside, she glanced over her shoulder.

Marshall was still there, waiting for her.

He grinned. "I'll be right here."

Tamara said nothing, just escaped into the bathroom. Once inside, she headed directly to the sink, turned on the faucet and then splashed her face with cold water.

Tamara raised her head and looked at her reflection. Not

only did she feel out of sorts, she looked a little flushed. She didn't think she had overdone it with the alcohol, but perhaps the punch had pushed her over the edge.

For goodness' sake, what had she gotten herself into with Marshall? She hadn't expected him to be like a dog with a bone.

"He sees this whole thing as a game," she said to her reflection. "He'll get bored soon enough."

She should have known that with a man like Marshall, once she had taken on the role of the mouse, he would take on the role of the cat.

Taking one of the hand towels from a wicker basket, she delicately dried her face. She was feeling even more light-headed than minutes ago and wondered if she was coming down with something.

She went into a stall and then came out and washed her hands. Perhaps she should just put Marshall out of his misery now. Tell him that she knew who he was because he had played this very game with her cousin. And she'd heard about him with other women, as well.

The Marshall she had known years ago had loved the chase. And he was good at conquering.

All of the time spent with him this evening had proved to Tamara that he hadn't changed over the years.

The heir to the auto fortune that his father had built, Marshall went after women as though it was a sport. Callie told her that he'd never been married. He was what now—thirty-four, thirty-five? It wasn't a crime to be single at that age, but Tamara would bet her last dollar that Marshall didn't want to settle down because he didn't believe in commitment.

Which had actually made him a perfect candidate for flirting with tonight. Their banter had been entertaining and had totally kept her from thinking about Patrick.

She exited the bathroom, noting that she seemed to be walking a little bit unsteadily. As promised, Marshall was standing there, waiting.

Her eyes roamed over him from head to toe. The black suit that looked like a million dollars on him. He truly was one incredibly fine specimen of a man. There was no doubt as to why the women swooned over him.

"You want to get to know me better," Tamara said without preamble as she walked toward him. "Really get to know me?"

"Absolutely."

"Then how's this?" None too gracefully, she closed the distance between them. And as she eased up on her toes, the thought that came into her mind was that she was definitely drunk. Because she had no clue why she was doing what she was doing...nor could she stop herself.

Completely out of character, Tamara tipped up on her toes and planted her lips firmly on his. She gripped his shoulders, more for support than anything, and after about five seconds, she ended the kiss as quickly as she had initiated it.

Easing back, she looked up at Marshall. Saw the confusion on his face. And felt it in herself as her head swam.

Why'd she just do that?

Marshall's expression said that he was stunned but also delighted. He raised an eyebrow. "Wow."

"That's what you wanted, isn't it?" she asked, her tongue feeling heavy. "To score?"

"Come again?"

She took a step backward, swaying unsteadily. "I gave you what you wanted, so now you can move on. The chase is over."

Marshall frowned. "You kiss me like that, and then you tell me..."

Tamara didn't hear the rest of what Marshall was saying, because the room began to spin violently. She reached out but there was nothing to grab onto.

"Tamara?" she heard him say.

The last conscious memory she had was of strong arms encircling her waist.

And then the world went black.

* * *

Holding Tamara's limp body in his arms, Marshall looked down at her with a sense of disbelief. What the heck had just happened?

Her eyes were closed and her plump lips were slightly parted. She was undoubtedly out cold.

Marshall felt for a pulse. It was there, and it was strong. Her breathing was shallow but steady.

He had seen this before. Women who drank too much. Suddenly, the alcohol hit them, and they passed out.

The weird thing was, she hadn't exhibited any signs of being inebriated earlier. She hadn't lost her footing on the dance floor, and her speech hadn't been slurred. It had been only moments before she faltered that he'd realized something was wrong.

"Tamara," he called softly. She said nothing.

He scooped her up into his arms and carried her toward the nearby sofa. He sat her down beside him and propped her head against his shoulder. "Tamara?" he said again.

All he heard in response was the sound of her breathing.

She hadn't taken something in the bathroom, had she? Some sort of drug? It was a crazy idea, and one Marshall dismissed. She didn't seem like the type.

He touched her face. She was warm. Her skin was smooth. His eyes ventured a little lower, over her thighs and down her legs. At the silver sandals on her delicate feet.

Wow, she was gorgeous.

And she was an enigma. Why had she kissed him? Oh, he had no complaints. Not until she'd said that whole thing about scoring and giving him what he wanted.

She had no clue what he wanted, and he wondered why she had judged him so harshly.

"Tamara?" He lightly tapped her face and still got no response.

It was clear to him that she wasn't waking up anytime soon. Marshall didn't know if he should leave her on this sofa and go to find Nigel. He was about to do just that, then considered the fact that Nigel had told him that the boys were staying with the babysitter for the evening. It wouldn't exactly be the best thing for Nigel to bring Tamara back there, possibly have her son see her in this state.

Marshall would take her to his place. He would watch her, see if her vital signs changed and act accordingly if they did. But he suspected that the alcohol had simply caught up with her and all she needed was to sleep it off. Then, in the morning, he would bring her home.

Yeah, that seemed like the best thing to do. Besides, the reception was still in full swing, and he didn't want to take Nigel or Callie or any of the family away from the festivities. His cousin had already left, so there was nothing keeping him here at this point.

Tamara moved against him, snuggling her head against his shoulder a little. A smile touched Marshall's lips. Did she have any clue what she was doing? That she was with him now? At least she appeared content.

A sleeping angel.

Marshall reached into his jacket pocket for his cell phone, and he sent Nigel a text explaining what he was going to do. He told him not to worry, that he would handle the situation and that Tamara would be returned safe and sound in the morning.

For good measure, he added: Don't worry. She's in good hands. I'm heeding your warning.

Then Marshall pulled Tamara's delicate body onto his lap and secured his arms beneath her legs and around her shoulders. He began to walk with her toward the establishment's main doors, garnering some stares from a few people nearby.

Marshall grinned at an older couple and said, "Don't worry, folks. I'm a police officer. I'm making sure that this young lady here gets home."

"Is she okay?" the older man asked.

"Yes," Marshall answered. "Just a little too much to drink. Nothing a night's rest won't cure."

As he looked down at the sleeping beauty in his arms, he thought again about the way she had kissed him.

And how he was very much looking forward to doing it again.

Chapter 4

Tamara awoke startled. Her eyes flew open, suddenly registering that something wasn't right.

She wasn't in her bed. She realized that even before her eyes started flitting around the room. No, this four-poster bed was most definitely not her own. Just as panic was about to set in, she remembered that she was in Cleveland, not Fort Lauderdale. Of course she wasn't in her bed.

But even as she remembered that, the sense that something was wrong persisted. Because she couldn't remember ever stepping into Callie and Nigel's house, much less getting under the covers.

And something else was strange. By the way the bedsheet was skimming her body, she could tell she wasn't wearing a bra. She'd been so exhausted that she had taken off her clothes and climbed into bed without even putting on her nightgown?

It was as if her brain had gone blank. She closed her eyes tightly and tried to concentrate. She was in Cleveland. She'd been at Deanna's wedding, which had been last night. Yes, that was right. Callie had forced her onto the dance floor to participate in the bouquet toss.

Tamara's eyes popped open. The bouquet. Marshall. Their dance.

Then she'd gone to the restroom, and he'd followed her.

And then, a kiss? She gasped. Oh, God. No, that couldn't be right.

As her stomach fluttered with the wisp of a memory, she wondered why the house was so quiet. The clock on the night table told her it was 9:18 a.m. Shouldn't Michael and Kwame be up and making noise?

Tamara surveyed the large bedroom, with its pale green walls, dresser with mirror and...*fireplace?* Nigel and Callie had a spare bedroom with a fireplace? The TV mounted to the wall was at least forty inches. There was a leather love seat beside the window, and through the sheer drapes she could see a sprawling tree outside.

The room boasted polished hardwood floors. But nowhere upon them did she see her suitcases.

She looked around the room again, this time with a sense of desperation. It was minimalist in terms of the furnishings and the decor. Spotting a framed photo on the far corner of the dresser, her eyes soon widened in alarm.

Was that *Marshall?*

Where was she?

The next second, her stomach filled with dread as she added up the reality in her mind. Marshall's picture, the lack of suitcases, the absence of any voices...

No, it couldn't be...

She couldn't actually be in Marshall's bed!

Her brain scrambled to make sense of the situation. The wedding. The reception. Flirting with Marshall.

"Oh, God," she uttered in horror. She remembered the kiss again. *She* had kissed *him.* Oh, yes, that had definitely happened. She remembered her mouth connecting with his full lips. It hadn't been the longest kiss, but she felt it throughout her entire body.

What had happened *after* that kiss?

And why was she in his bed without her clothes on?

"God, please tell me I didn't. Please tell me I didn't do something incredibly stupid!"

But she was beginning to fear that she had. If she had come into this bed merely to sleep, wouldn't her dress be neatly draped over that rocking chair? She couldn't see it anywhere.

Finally, she bent her head to look over the side of the bed. And her mortification intensified. Because there was her dress, in a heap on the floor. As though it had been discarded haphazardly.

"I can't possibly be…"

And then for some reason, she craned her neck to look over her shoulder. And on the wall she saw a photo of Marshall with his parents and brother. A family portrait.

There was no longer any doubt. She was in Marshall's house.

In his room.

In his bed.

Her horror level reached a 10.0 on the Richter scale.

Oh God, oh God, oh God! What have I done?

The house was still quiet, and Tamara prayed that Marshall was in a bathroom somewhere. If she could get up quietly, she could sneak out of the house.

She threw the covers off of the queen-size bed and slipped her legs over the side. As her feet came down on the floor, the hardwood squeaked. She winced, hoping that she didn't get Marshall's attention—wherever he was in the house. Because she had to get out of there without him knowing.

She didn't even know where he lived in relation to Callie and Nigel, but she would find her way somehow. Maybe Marshall was the type who had to work out every morning, and that was where he was now. If so, all the better.

She couldn't face him.

She'd been in his bed. And she knew what Marshall did

with women in his bed. Even if she hadn't heard the salacious stories, the fact that her dress had been tossed onto the floor spoke volumes.

But why couldn't she remember anything? Somehow, she had lost time. She remembered... She remembered nothing. The kiss, yes.

But certainly not a hot night between the sheets.

She quickly scooped her dress up from the floor and slipped it onto her body. Then she reached for the zipper on the side and pulled it up. The mauve dress with swirls of white had looked incredibly sexy on her when she'd put it on, and that had been what she'd needed. As a newly divorced woman, she'd wanted to look feminine and desirable.

And she had—to Marshall. Had this very dress led her down the path of temptation and into this dilemma? She had wanted to reclaim her womanhood. Had she done that and more?

And with Marshall, of all people?

Tamara opened the bedroom door and peered into the house at large, finding that she was in the hallway. On the opposite side she saw that the door to another bedroom was open. It was much larger, with a king-size poster bed, and far more photos on the wall. Clearly, that was Marshall's master bedroom.

Realizing that she hadn't been in his bed should have given her comfort. But it didn't. Because his bed was immaculately spread and didn't look as though it had been slept in last night.

She swallowed and then stepped to her left, toward the top of a staircase. The staircase opened up to a two-story ceiling, with a large skylight. Sunlight flooded into the house, almost like a spotlight on her as she made her way down the stairs. The steps creaked, and she tried to tiptoe without making much sound but it was pointless.

Where was Marshall? In another bedroom? She didn't hear the shower.

The house appeared massive, with a huge great room off of the foyer. She could see the brown-leather sectional, with decorative throw pillows, in front of a wall that housed a television that looked to be sixty inches. As she stepped onto the first-floor landing, she could see part of a dining-room table in a room that sprang from the left of the foyer. The wood was black, probably black maple, and the room had majestic gold-colored curtains topped with cream swags. It was the kind of house Tamara would love to explore, but given the circumstances, she just wanted to get out as quickly as possible.

Tamara's feet were cold on the marble floor, but thank God her silver stiletto sandals were neatly sitting on a mat near the door. And she saw her purse on the table in the foyer. At least she would have her phone to call for a taxi and money to pay for it.

A house like this would have an alarm, and she only prayed that it wasn't currently set. The small alarm panel was closer to the door, so she hurried over to it and perused it, determining with relief that it didn't appear to be activated.

She bent over and slipped her bare foot into one shoe. She was putting on the second shoe when the door began to open. Her heart spasmed.

In walked Marshall. As though he had walked into his house to greet her in the morning countless times, he smiled an easy, charming smile. Was that the smile he had used last night to get what he wanted?

"You're up," he said. And then a little frown marred his face. "Where are you going?"

"I—I have to leave. My son—Michael—he'll be… God, I can't believe this."

She was flustered, and she couldn't form coherent words. The last thing she wanted was to be heading back to Callie's place the morning after some sort of scandalous night with Marshall. Her son would wonder where she had been, and what could she tell him?

Lord, this was a nightmare.

"I picked up some breakfast," Marshall told her. "I didn't have anything decent in the house. I bought some egg sandwiches from a local deli. A few varieties, since I didn't know what you liked. I got coffee, too." He lifted the tray in his hands, in case she somehow hadn't seen it.

"I'm not hungry."

"It's never a good idea to skip breakfast," Marshall said.

"Thank you for…" She stiffened. For what? "I—I need to get to my son."

"You can't take a few minutes to eat breakfast with me?" His eyes narrowed slightly, saying he was more than a little confused as to why she wanted to get out of his house so fast.

She supposed she could understand why he was confused. Most women probably didn't run screaming from him the morning after a night spent in his bed.

But she wasn't most women. And clearly, she wasn't even herself. She had no memory of what had happened at all, which made it much worse.

"I'm sorry," Tamara said. "I'd rather just leave."

"Are you sure?"

"Yes. I need to get to my son. This is not how I planned our first night in Cleveland to be." She was flustered. She stared up at him, her chest rapidly moving with each breath. "But thank you. Thank you for the coffee and the breakfast sandwich."

"Are you okay?" Marshall asked.

That was a loaded question. How could she be okay? She didn't know what she'd done with him, but she could only imagine the worst. She didn't dare ask him, like some fool who ended up in a man's bed with no recollection of it. Obviously, she'd had too much alcohol and had somehow passed out.

She forced a smile but barely met his gaze. "I'm fine. I'll take the coffee and sandwich with me for later, if you don't mind."

Marshall nodded. "Sure. Though I'm a little disappointed that you want to get away from me so quickly this morning."

Again, the smile. This time a little devilish. Tamara's stomach sank.

She'd slept with him. It was obvious now. The look in his eyes, she knew she had.

Oh, God.

Tamara took a coffee from the tray. "I'll just call for a taxi. No need for you to take me to Callie and Nigel's place."

"Don't be silly. I'll drive you."

Tamara felt a bout of anxiety. She wanted to escape Marshall, not be confined in a closed space with him. "It's perfectly fine. You've already…done enough."

"Their house is in Shaker Heights, about a fifteen-minute drive," he told her. "Honestly, how long will it take a taxi to get here when you call? I'll just take you."

Tamara hadn't thought of that, and certainly it didn't make sense to sit or stand inside or on the porch for possibly ten minutes or longer for a taxi to arrive. She would love nothing more than to simply flee, start walking *anywhere,* but she'd caught sight of his sprawling circular driveway when he'd opened the door. Heck, it would probably take her five minutes to get off of his property—where on earth would she walk to?

As much as she wanted to be away from Marshall, taking him up on his offer for a ride seemed the best thing to do.

"As long as you don't have anything else to do," Tamara said, resigned to her fate.

"I'm all yours."

Tamara cringed at the words, wondering if they held special meaning for him. Then she opened the cutout in her coffee lid and sipped it.

"I got it with a little cream and a little sugar," Marshall explained. "I didn't know how you would like it."

"This is fine." She stepped toward the front door. "I don't want to rush you, but if you're ready to leave…"

"Sure."

Tamara stepped out the door, which was almost flush with the ground, then waited for Marshall to join her. "Hold this for me?" he asked, offering her the bag with the sandwiches and the coffee tray.

Tamara took the items while he closed the door. She checked out the breadth of his shoulders, clad in a T-shirt this morning, and she noted that he was just as sexy in casual wear as he had been in his suit yesterday.

He turned to face her, and she quickly averted her eyes.

He took the coffee and bag from her and then started toward the car with an easy and sexy gait. Tamara followed him to the sleek, black BMW. She didn't remember being in it last night, but she must have been.

What else had she done?

Marshall opened the passenger door for her, then went around and got in on the driver's side. Tamara was about to get into the car when she saw a cushion on the seat covered with blond hair.

"What?" Marshall asked, looking up at her.

"Is that *dog hair?*"

Marshall grabbed the cushion and tossed it into the backseat. "Sorry, yeah."

Tamara looked around anxiously, half expecting some giant fur ball to be lunging toward her. "You have a dog?"

"It's a buddy's dog. He's gone for the weekend, asked me to check in on him. So I picked Sherlock up this morning and took her to the park so she could run laps with me."

Tamara still stood there, not getting into the car.

"I already brought Sherlock home," Marshall said. "What, you don't like dogs?"

"Not particularly," Tamara admitted. She had delivered flyers as a teen. More than one dog had chased her or barked savagely at her.

"Well, Sherlock's at home." Marshall dusted the leather seat to get any stray dog hairs off. "Will you just get in the car?"

With a sigh, Tamara did just that. Marshall then started the car, and loud hip-hop immediately blared through the speakers. Marshall reached for the volume control and turned it down.

Tamara said nothing, just sipped her coffee as a way of avoiding having to speak. She was desperate to find out what had happened the night before, and also terrified. She knew it was very likely that she had behaved inappropriately, but she was embarrassed to ask.

Perhaps there was a part of her that needed that kind of wild encounter with someone to help make her feel desirable again. It had been a while since she'd been with any man. And as much as it was clearly out of character for her to engage in a one-night stand, obviously, on some level, she'd needed to get it on with someone.

"So," Marshall began, "did you have a good time yesterday?"

Tamara's stomach twisted. Was he talking about the wedding? Or afterward? Tamara looked at him briefly and then averted her gaze. "If you mean at the wedding," she said pointedly, "yes, it was lovely."

"What do you think I mean?" Marshall asked.

"I—I don't... I didn't..." Tamara's voice trailed off.

"I'm a trained investigator," Marshall told her. When Tamara glanced at him, she saw that he was giving her a curious look. "It's obvious there's something else on your mind."

Tamara said nothing.

"Tamara?" She could feel Marshall's eyes on her. "Why don't you tell—"

"Look," she interrupted him, releasing a heavy breath as she stared at him. "I'll make this clear. Whatever happened last night, it can't happen again. I mean, here I am in your car after a night at your house that I don't even remember. This isn't like me. I do—" She faltered. "I do remember kissing you. And then...I wake up half-naked in your bed?"

Marshall's eyes widened, as though intrigued. "You don't remember what happened?"

"No. Which tells me I obviously wasn't in my right mind. And you...*you* should have known better, even if I didn't."

"So that's why you seem on edge," he said, sounding as though he finally got it.

For someone who touted himself as a trained investigator, he was also a little dense.

"Of course that's why I'm on edge," Tamara responded, her words a little harsher than she'd intended. "I'm not the kind of woman you typically date."

"How would you know the kind of woman I typically date?"

"It's obvious."

"Really?" Marshall sounded amused. "How is it obvious?"

Tamara had started something, something she wished she hadn't. She should have just kept her mouth shut. Moved on from the mistake of the night before and forgotten it ever happened.

"Come on. You say something like that, you've got to explain yourself. I met you last night. How on earth can you act as if you know me?"

"Didn't you start off at the wedding with someone else?" Tamara raised an eyebrow as if she had just scored a match point.

"My cousin, Renee. I told you that."

"Right," Tamara scoffed. "She looked like she just came from the Playboy mansion."

"She is beautiful. And she's also my cousin. I wouldn't lie about that."

Tamara glanced at Marshall. He appeared truthful. Which only made her feel even dumber than getting so drunk the night before that she didn't remember a thing.

But the truth was, she knew of Marshall's reputation. He could pretend to be a choirboy, and maybe he had changed, but life had taught her that people didn't just transform into better versions of themselves. She had married Patrick, ignoring his early bouts of jealousy, thinking he would calm down once he felt secure with the reality that she was his wife. Instead, Patrick's behavior had only intensified.

Marshall had always had a reputation as being a ladies' man, and she didn't imagine that that would have changed throughout the years. The fact that she'd ended up at his house, in his bed, did more to prove he was the same man he'd been thirteen years ago.

"The fact that you took me home last night speaks volumes," Tamara said.

"Does it, now?" Marshall asked.

"In my state of mind? Of course it does." She still didn't understand how she'd gotten so drunk, but that was a moot point now. "But I'm just letting you know that whatever happened, it was a one-time thing. I'm not the sort of woman who hooks up with men for one-night stands. That is totally *not* me."

Marshall nodded slowly. "I see."

"I suspect that'll suit you just fine anyway," she added in a voice that was almost a whisper.

"Excuse me?"

With a huge sense of relief, Tamara started to recognize her old neighborhood. "Oh, thank God. We're almost there."

"Can't wait to get away from me," Marshall commented, sounding as though he was speaking to himself. "I guess I should be offended."

Tamara didn't respond, just sipped her coffee. She wished she could be out of the car already.

Away from Marshall.

Maybe it was better that she had no recollection of last night. Even if all she and Marshall had done last night was fool around a little, it was still too much for her liking. Not knowing the details, she could pretend that nothing had happened.

Sure, it wasn't the most mature way to look at things, but she didn't particularly feel like being an adult about this. Because as she neared Callie and Nigel's house, she was wondering how on earth she was going to explain herself to her son and to her friends.

Minutes later, Marshall slowed and turned into the driveway of Callie and Nigel's home and pulled up behind Tamara's car. Yesterday, between the wedding and the reception, Tamara had followed Callie to the house when she'd brought the boys to the sitter, and they had gone to the reception hall in one car. Tamara was extremely grateful she'd had the foresight to do that, which saved her from having to head back to the reception hall this morning.

As Marshall put the car into Park, Tamara began to undo the seat belt immediately. But as she reached to open the door with her other hand, Marshall took her gently by the wrist.

She looked at him. "What are you doing?"

"You don't want to ask me what happened last night? You don't want to know?" he said as he released her wrist.

Tamara swallowed. She wanted to know, but then again she didn't want to know. Her chest tightened with anxiety even while her stomach fluttered with a different sensation.

"Whatever happened, I think it's best that we for—"

"Forget it. Fine."

Marshall's response gave Tamara pause. Guilt made her stomach tense. She was being harsh with him, and he looked as though he had no clue why.

It was time she fill him in. "You dated my cousin," she told him. "That's how I know all about you. I'm not passing judgment out of thin air."

Marshall's eyes narrowed with confusion. "What?"

"Twelve years ago—thirteen, actually—you dated my cousin, and you broke her heart. Gloria Miller?" she added, when he continued to seem clueless. "You chased her, you got what you wanted and then you dumped her. She was crushed. And she wasn't the only woman you used and abused. There were plenty. Your reputation…it was pretty infamous."

Understanding filled Marshall's eyes. "Ahh, so that explains your attitude." He paused. "Then the kiss last night…?"

"Was a bit of payback. I was toying with you. Letting you know that you can't get your way with every woman. The kiss was about…teaching you a lesson." Tamara quickly looked downward, shame coming over her. Some lesson that had been.

"At least now I know why you think ill of me. But clearly, whatever lesson you wanted to teach me didn't go exactly as planned."

Tamara whipped her gaze to his. "I realize that! You don't have to rub it in."

Several seconds passed, seconds that seemed like hours. Marshall stared at her, and Tamara held his gaze, determined not to let her embarrassment get to her.

"I really do need to get inside."

"And here I thought we'd made some sort of connection last night. I mean, that kiss didn't feel like payback..."

"You need me to spell it out? I'm not interested. Not in a guy like you."

"Ouch."

"Okay," Tamara said, breathing out harshly. "This has gone in a direction I never intended. Please, let's just forget all of it. I apologize for being offensive. Obviously things got to a certain level between us last night and I'm upset about that. And now I keep putting my foot in my mouth. I'm embarrassed enough."

"I'm not stopping you from leaving," Marshall said.

"Thank you." Tamara opened the door.

But as she was stepping out the car, Marshall said, "Though you might want to know that you don't need to be embarrassed. At least not about what did or did not happen last night."

Tamara halted but didn't look at him.

"I have no clue how you got naked, because when I put you in my spare bedroom, you had your dress on. You must have taken it off some time in the night."

Tamara spun around and faced him, her breaths coming rapidly.

"A beautiful woman like you—would I have wanted to help you out of your dress? Sure, if you had been conscious and willing. But you were out cold, and I put you in the spare bed so that you could get some rest and sleep it off."

Tamara's eyes widened as she searched his face. "You're saying that we never—"

"No." His eyes held hers for a long moment. "Not that I wouldn't have been willing," he added, and the words alone made her feel flushed. "But since you practically passed out in my arms when you came out of the restroom, and because I didn't want to bother Callie or Nigel with the situation—or to have you go home in that state and have your son see you—I took you to my place."

Tamara was stunned; she had no clue what to say. Not only had he not taken advantage of her, he'd actually been thinking of her son—something she greatly appreciated.

"Never in my life have I had to take advantage of a woman to get her into my bed, and I'm not about to start now."

"You—you never took off my dress?" How had she gotten naked, then? She must have awoken, perhaps because she was hot. Yes, she had memories of being hot. She must have taken off her own dress and had no recollection of it.

"I guess you'll believe what you want to believe," Marshall said. "But, Tamara, the truth is that I didn't touch you in an inappropriate way. As amusing as it was to watch you squirm, believing that we'd made love, I wanted to make sure that you knew nothing happened—since the idea of sharing my bed bothers you that much."

"I—I'm sorry." It was the only thing Tamara could say, even though she knew the words wouldn't be enough. "I…I just… I thought… I really am sorry."

She'd been flustered. Out of her element. On edge around Marshall.

"Nigel is my best friend," Marshall explained. "I told him last night I was going to take you home, look out for you. And even if you think I wouldn't care about taking advantage of you, there's no way that I would disrespect Nigel and the trust he placed in me. You can take that to the bank."

Tamara felt like a heel. "Like I said, I'm sorry. I don't get drunk, and I still don't understand what happened. Waking up in a strange bed had me out of sorts. So, I apologize for my attitude. And thank you," she added faintly.

"Pardon me?"

Tamara couldn't meet Marshall's eyes. If she never had to

see him again, it would be too soon. Her humiliation was at an all-time high.

She drew in a deep breath and faced him. Hadn't she dealt with much worse in her life? "Thank you," she said more firmly, meaning it. "Thank you for looking out for me last night when I couldn't do it myself."

"You're welcome. And a word of advice? Lay off the alcohol."

Tamara's face flamed. "Maybe it was something in one of the drinks. Or maybe it was the fatigue of driving for two days. Or maybe…" Her voice trailed off as it suddenly hit her. Why hadn't she thought of it before?

"What?" Marshall asked.

"Gin," she said. "There must have been gin in the punch. I've never liked it, and the one time I had it in college, I had a bad reaction and passed out. Of course." It all made sense now.

She'd had the punch, felt weird in the bathroom and then couldn't remember anything beyond the kiss. The truth was, she was lucky Marshall had been with her at the time she'd blacked out. She would have been far more horrified to know that she had passed out on the floor and was found by another guest at the reception.

"Gin, huh?" Marshall asked.

"I thought the punch would have champagne, not gin." Tamara shook her head, wishing she could undo what had happened, but knowing that it could be much worse. "Thank you, again. I mean that."

"Anytime."

Tamara offered Marshall a weak smile. She knew her apology wouldn't undo the words she'd said, but it was the best she had to offer.

She placed her hand on the door and was just about to close it when Marshall suddenly lifted the brown bag with the sandwiches and extended it to her. "Don't forget your breakfast."

"Oh. Right. Thanks."

Tamara took the bag, and then the coffee, which he handed

her next. She closed the door and stepped away from the car, giving him a little wave as she did.

Then she started toward the house and didn't dare look back as she heard the car pull out of the driveway.

Chapter 5

Tamara turned the knob for the front door and found it open. She had hoped that she could step into the house and find everyone still in bed. But instead, she found the opposite. She heard a house filled with chatter.

She slipped out of her shoes in the foyer before walking the short distance to the living room. Kwame and Michael were sitting on the edge of the sofa with Xbox controllers in their hands and didn't immediately see her. As she stepped farther into the living room and the kitchen came into view, Tamara saw Callie and Nigel sitting at the table, both with empty plates of breakfast and coffee mugs before them.

"Mom!" Michael exclaimed, finally noticing her. He dropped his controller, ran toward her and threw his arms around her waist. It was as if she had been gone for a week, instead of just the night.

Tamara slipped her arm around her son's body and pulled him close. "Hey, honey."

"Where were you?" Michael asked.

"I...I was at a friend of Nigel's," she answered. "He's a

police officer," she added, to relieve her son of any possible misgivings. "I ate something that didn't agree with me, and I wasn't feeling well, so Nigel's friend took me back to his place and let me sleep there."

"Why didn't you just come back here?" Michael asked.

"Because I didn't want to worry you. I figured you were having a blast with Kwame, and if I came back here, sick, you would have been worried. The good news is I feel a lot better now." She smiled to prove her point.

"Everyone was wondering where you were," Michael explained.

"Well, here I am, and I'm perfectly fine." Tamara kissed Michael on the forehead. "Hey, Kwame." As she released her son, she went over to give Kwame a hug.

"Hi, Aunt Tamara," Kwame said, his embrace long and warm. Though she wasn't his biological aunt, he addressed her that way, and Michael addressed Callie as his aunt, as well.

The boys went back to their game, and Tamara started for the kitchen. Callie's eyes were already alight as she made her way in there, as though she believed her friend had a story to tell.

"My, my, my," Callie said in a singsong voice. "She lives."

"I live." Tamara placed her bag of breakfast and coffee cup on the table and then took a seat beside Callie. "Morning, Callie. Nigel."

"Good morning," Nigel greeted her.

"Is there still coffee?" Tamara asked. "I'll need another one soon."

"Yep," Callie answered. "There's a half a pot left."

Tamara opened the brown paper bag and pulled out one of the two bagel-and-egg sandwiches. She was distinctly aware of Callie's eyes on her as she did. Looking at her friend, she asked, "What?"

"Oh, I'm just waiting for you to tell me what happened."

Tamara unwrapped one of the sandwiches. "There's nothing to tell. Nothing that I can remember, in any case."

"So you really passed out?" Callie asked in a low tone, almost sounding disappointed.

"What—you thought that was some story Marshall made up?" Tamara countered.

"Well, you did catch the bouquet, Marshall caught the garter, and right after you two danced, you disappeared together."

Tamara's eyes widened in alarm. She hoped no one else had jumped to the same conclusion her friend had. "I assure you, it's not what you think."

"That's what I told her," Nigel said.

"No," Tamara reiterated emphatically. "Definitely not. I have no clue how, but apparently I passed out and Marshall happened to be there when I did, and he took me to his place because he didn't want me coming back here in an unconscious state…." She indicated the boys with a jerk of her head over her shoulder. "Which was really nice of him, by the way. It saved Michael any undue stress."

"Yeah, Marshall's good people," Nigel concurred.

"Then I woke up, and Marshall brought me right here," Tamara summarized.

"After you stopped for breakfast, you mean." Callie gestured to the egg bagel.

"No. Marshall went out when I was still sleeping and picked up breakfast. By the time he got back, I was already up and ready to leave."

"And that's it?" Callie pressed, raising a suspicious eyebrow.

"Callie," Nigel said in a mildly chiding tone, "stop giving Tamara a hard time."

"It's just that…both of you looked like you were getting real cozy on the dance floor."

"You mean when I danced with him because the entire room expected me to?" Tamara countered. "I was just doing the polite thing."

"Oh." Callie's lips turned downward in a small frown.

"Marshall said you were completely out of it," Nigel commented. "He was worried until you started shifting around and muttering in your sleep around two in the morning. He didn't go to bed until he knew you were okay."

The words gave Tamara pause. Had Marshall been sitting in the room watching her? "Really?" she asked.

"He's trained as a paramedic," Nigel explained. "He was able to monitor your vital signs and determine if you needed care at a hospital. But," Nigel went on, his eyes twinkling with a bit of humor, "he figured you'd had too much to drink and merely needed to sleep it off."

"I'm so embarrassed," Tamara said. "That's totally not like me."

"You've had a rough time lately," Nigel said. "No one can blame you."

"The thing is, I think I had a reaction to what was in the punch." Tamara faced Callie. "Remember in college, when I had gin that time and passed out? It was the only time in my life that had happened."

Callie began to nod. "Yes, that's right."

"I was feeling fine until I went and had some of the punch. Next thing I know, I was starting to feel weird. Then I wake up in a strange house.... I think there must have been gin in the punch."

"That's your story, and you're sticking to it." Callie smiled sweetly.

"Stop!" Tamara protested. "I'm being serious."

"I'm just razzing you," Callie said, then squeezed her hand. "I'm happy you're here. And that you're okay. And mostly, I'm happy that I can tease you about last night—rather than deal with a much heavier topic around this breakfast table."

Tamara exhaled a calming breath. "Yes," she said, nodding. "You're absolutely right."

"I'll leave you two ladies to chat," Nigel said, rising. "Tamara, if your cup is empty, I can put some coffee in it for you."

"Oh, sure." Tamara passed Nigel her cup. "Thank you."

Several seconds later, he was passing her the cup. "The milk, cream and sugar is right on the table."

"I noticed. Thanks again."

"No problem."

Tamara set about adding sugar and cream to her coffee. "I have to tell you, when I woke up, I had no clue where I was. And I was seriously shocked to realize I was in Marshall's place."

"I'll bet. But now that Nigel's gotten up, you can tell me. Was there a small part of you that was secretly thrilled when you realized you were at his place?"

Tamara's eyes widened. "No. *No.* Why would you say that?"

"You've seen Marshall, haven't you? The man is seriously fine. Of course, I'm partial to Nigel, but Marshall's a good catch."

"What?" Tamara asked.

"He's hot. And he's single."

Tamara was flabbergasted. "You're not suggesting… No, I know you're not."

"What, is it wrong for me to be a little hopeful where you and Marshall are concerned? Sometimes, I think there's something in the water here in Cleveland. Something good, girl. My sisters and I came back here and we all found love. And I thought I saw something between you and Marshall last night."

Tamara was too stunned to speak.

"I *know* I saw some flirting going on," Callie stressed. "Before you caught the bouquet."

Tamara stiffened her back. "It was a festive occasion—maybe I flirted a little. No big deal."

"Well, no matter what happens, good for you," Callie said. "I'm happy to know that you had a good time. You've had an awful year, and you deserve to have a little flirtatious fun."

Tamara eyed her friends skeptically. "Maybe you're right about that whole something being in the water here in Cleveland. Because you certainly have this whole romantic aura about you that I don't remember from before."

Callie shrugged. "What can I say? I'm happy, Tamara." She glanced over her shoulder at Nigel, who was sitting on the sofa between the boys, and beamed. "Really and truly happy. And who knows what fate has in store for you?"

Tamara shook her head. "Oh, no. Fate's got a whole other plan in store for me. And it has nothing to do with a man. I'm here to take a step back from dating and concentrate on rebuilding my life. Getting involved with a man is the last thing I need to do."

"I'm just saying, be open to whatever might happen."

Tamara didn't know why Callie was so convinced Marshall might be good for her, and it was time to set her straight. "Definitely not with Marshall," Tamara said. "I remember him—and his reputation—from years ago. He dated one of my cousins. After pursuing her relentlessly. She thought he was cute but heard he was a player, so she was skeptical. Marshall broke down her defenses, and once he got what he wanted, he broke her heart."

Callie frowned. "Oh. Well, that sucks."

"Yeah. So even if I were looking, Marshall would be the last guy I wanted."

"For what it's worth, I think he's changed a lot over the years. I haven't seen the player side of him—of course, I'm not paying attention to that—but I do know that he gives back his time to the community and donates to a lot of great causes. His family—"

"—owns a number of car dealerships," Tamara finished for her. "Which made him all the more attractive. Every girl knew that he came from money."

"No doubt. I'm sure a lot of women were after him for all the wrong reasons."

"And for a guy like Marshall—at least eleven, twelve years ago—that kind of attention was what he wanted. He's good for a fling, but nothing else."

Tamara suddenly registered the last words she'd said, and her stomach grew queasy. *He's good for a fling, but nothing else.* Why had those words come from her mouth?

"Not that I mean… I'm not saying…" Tamara sputtered.

Callie grinned at her. "So you've thought about it?"

"No. Of course not. I don't even know why I said that."

"Relax," Callie told her. "I know what you mean." She paused for a moment. "But I suppose if you ever wanted… a little something…Marshall would be very good at…*that*."

Callie giggled, and Tamara lifted the egg sandwich to her mouth. But as she took a bite, all she could think about was the way Marshall had looked at her the night before.

She had no doubt that he'd be good in bed. No doubt at all.

Hours passed since Marshall had dropped Tamara off. And though Marshall had done a serious kickboxing workout in hopes of freeing his mind, he was still thinking about her.

The look on her face when she had started to tell him that what had happened between them could never happen again had been priceless.

Sure, Marshall could have set her straight before he did. But it had been amusing to watch her squirm. All while trying to figure out the beautiful enigma who had come into his life.

She had flirted with him, then pulled away. She had kissed him, then passed out. Come the morning, he had hoped for the playful, flirtatious Tamara, but instead, she had been mortified to see him.

She had been trying to escape his house when he'd entered, which wasn't something he was used to. Women who woke up in his house typically wanted to secure drawer space for themselves.

So as much as he'd been amused by her obvious discomfort in the morning, it had also been disheartening. Because the incredibly beautiful and vivacious woman who had teased him with one hell of a kiss the night before looked downright devastated at the idea that she had slept with him.

That wasn't exactly good for his ego.

Nor did it bode well for his hope that he could get to know her better.

Marshall would try not to take it personally, however. Nigel had told him about what had happened to her. So he knew that Tamara had gone through a tough time. An abusive husband who had tried to kill her, who had attacked and almost killed her best friend...that was a lot to deal with.

Didn't Marshall know it? As a cop, he'd handled domestic-abuse cases plenty of times. He knew the volatility of those relationships. He knew how often women were afraid to leave their abusers. How sometimes they would be ready to testify, only to cave as the moment came. Men who belittled their wives or girlfriends with words or physical beatings controlled them to an extent that many people didn't understand.

Why don't you just leave? was the common question that came from outsiders who couldn't understand why someone would stay with an abuser. There were no easy answers, but Marshall knew better than most just how difficult it was to disentangle yourself from someone you had been romantically involved with. He didn't doubt that Tamara had a deeply caring side to her, even though she hadn't shown it to him. But there was no doubt something about her ex-husband that had drawn out her nurturing side and inspired her to believe that she could help heal him.

It was all too common.

She had pegged him a player, and sure, there'd been a time when Marshall had enjoyed dating women and not committing. But what Tamara didn't know was why he hadn't been into commitment. She didn't know that it was his own devastating heartbreak that had led him to harden his heart.

Sixteen years ago, at the age of nineteen, he'd been head over heels in love with Vivica, his high school girlfriend. Vivica had enjoyed all of the finer things, which Marshall had bought her to keep her happy. When she went to California for college, Marshall paid for her flights back to Cleveland, and he went out to see her as much as possible.

One time, when he'd flown to California to surprise her, he'd been the one who'd gotten the surprise. Because in her dorm room, he'd found her with another man.

Marshall had been crushed. To learn that Vivica had been playing him for a fool while he'd continued to help her out with her living expenses... It had been a cold wake-up call that she had wanted him for his money.

Tamara had mentioned that he'd dated her cousin, Gloria, and that he'd dumped her after he'd gotten what he wanted. What Tamara didn't know was that Gloria had begun to exhibit the same characteristics as Vivica had, such as "I need this" and "Can you buy me that?" So Marshall had quickly ended his relationship with Gloria.

Besides, he hadn't truly been into her. With Gloria, he had been trying to pick up the pieces of his broken heart. Only a few months before meeting her, he had experienced loss again. And this time more devastating than with Vivica. He had been involved with someone like Tamara, someone who had been with an abuser. Lisa, unlike Vivica, had a vulnerable quality, and that had drawn him to her. Maybe there had even been a part of Marshall that had hoped to rescue her. All he knew then was that he hoped to pull her out from the darkness of her previous relationship. And he'd fallen for Lisa, who wanted nothing to do with his money. He'd fallen hard. She was beautiful; she was sweet. And she was fragile.

She had the exact kind of qualities he wanted his wife to possess. She was kind and nurturing, and he could see her being a fantastic mother. Love had hit him when he least expected it, and no one was more surprised than he. Seven months after they'd started dating, Marshall had been inspired to propose to her, believing it was the right thing and the right time.

Marshall had been happy when he asked her to marry him, but Lisa began to cry. And then she dealt the blow that broke his heart when she tearfully told him that she couldn't accept his proposal. Unbeknownst to Marshall, Lisa had been in touch with her ex. Andrew had apologized for not treating her right and begged her to forgive him. She hadn't been sure what to do, but Marshall proposing had made it clear to her that she couldn't marry a man she loved, but wasn't in love with.

So she went back to her ex.

With his love, Lisa had become a stronger woman. Or so he had believed. Obviously, he'd been wrong about believing she loved him, and the strength he thought she'd had had evaporated once her ex wanted her back.

Only months later Marshall had learned about her stabbing. Lisa died in hospital the day after the brutal attack.

Marshall thought of her often over the years, and always with pain in his heart. People thought he was this carefree playboy who didn't care to give his heart, but they didn't know. Only those closest to him knew of the pain he had endured.

Why was Marshall even thinking of Vivica and Lisa now, the two women who had broken his heart?

Because you're interested in Tamara.

Tamara was the first woman in a long time who had sparked his interest. Really sparked his interest. He wanted to get to know her on a much deeper level.

Which is stupid, he said to himself as he stepped into the shower at the gym. Marshall knew better than anyone else that there was a risk even thinking about getting involved with someone like Tamara. Tamara needed to rebuild herself first, come to a place of understanding about her past and her experiences, before she would ever be ready for a serious relationship.

He had learned that lesson with Lisa.

Knowing that Tamara needed to regain her confidence as a woman was the main reason why—though it had been tempting to let her believe she had been a wild, scandalous woman in his bed—he had instead allayed her concerns. He had told her that nothing had happened between them because he didn't want her to believe that there was a possibility that he had taken advantage of her. In her state, she needed security and reassurance that not all men were evil.

"She's off-limits, man," Marshall said as the warm water sluiced over his body. Nigel had said as much, and Marshall was determined to heed his friend's warning.

She was fragile, overcoming a serious life incident, and she didn't like dogs.

That was enough reason for him to stay away.

Chapter 6

On Monday, Tamara decided that she would take Michael around Cleveland. She would show him the neighborhood where she grew up, her old house, the schools she had attended. She hoped to familiarize him with the locale to help lessen any anxiety he might be feeling regarding their move to a new city.

Tamara had figured that just she and Michael would go for the ride, but when she suggested the idea, Kwame wanted to come along for the trip.

The more the merrier, as far as Tamara was concerned. Thus far, Michael and Kwame had reconnected as though no time had passed since they'd last seen each other. Which was great. Anything that would help take his mind off of the reality that his father was in jail.

Tamara asked Callie if she wanted to come along, as well, but she declined. With a whisper and an eyebrow wiggle, Callie said, "With all of you gone, I can have Nigel to myself for a while."

"Ahhh," Tamara said, understanding. "Gotcha."

Nigel wasn't due at work until the late afternoon. He was a detective, and he worked the late shift. From the few stories Tamara had heard since being here, it was a busy shift for homicide detectives.

Tamara winked at them on her way out of the house. "You two behave now."

Nigel slipped his arms around Callie's waist and drew her close. "Oh, we'll behave all right."

Tamara got into her car with the boys and they headed down to the waterfront. She was sure that Kwame and Michael wouldn't take in a single site as they busily played some game on their DS's in the backseat.

"Michael, this is Lake Erie," Tamara said, driving along it. "It's a big body of water, just like what you were used to in Florida."

"It looks superdark," Michael said.

"That's because this is a lake, not an ocean," Tamara explained. "Lakes are freshwater, compared to salt water. I love the blue of the Atlantic Ocean, but this water is perfectly fine for swimming. When we go to the beach, you'll notice that the sand is also darker than in Florida. Again, it's just different. But different doesn't mean bad."

"I know it looks dirty," Kwame began, "but it's actually clean, and it's lots of fun to go swimming there."

"That's right," Tamara agreed. "You'll probably prefer to get a mouthful of freshwater, as opposed to salt water. The bigger difference here is that you can't swim in this water for most of the year, whereas you can in Florida."

"But we get snow here," Kwame quickly chimed in. "And you'll love snow."

"I've always wanted to go tobogganing and stuff," Michael said.

"We definitely will," Tamara told him.

She showed him the various restaurants along the waterfront, and the marina. "This is one of the marinas."

"It reminds me of Florida," Michael said.

"Exactly," Tamara said. "It's a different state, but not all that different in many ways.

"This is the FirstEnergy Stadium," Tamara said, pointing it out as they approached the stadium, which was also on the water. "As you know, Aunt Natalie is married to a player from Cleveland."

"It's totally cool," Kwame said. "He took me to the stadium and into the locker rooms and everything."

"And that's the Great Lakes Science Center," Tamara said. She continued the waterfront tour by showing them the Rock and Roll Hall of Fame, before heading to a quaint part of the downtown area with boutique shops. From there, she went to her old neighborhood of Fairfax.

"Wow," Michael said as he looked around. "The houses are different here. They look really old."

"Yes, they're old, but these are beautiful Victorian homes with a lot of character," Tamara explained. "When I first went to Florida, I remember being amazed at how beautiful the architecture was. Everything was so bright and new. People used to joke that the houses in Florida were always new because a hurricane would come around every so often, knock everything down and force people to rebuild."

"None of the hurricanes ever knocked our house down!" Michael protested.

"I know, sweetie. The difference here is that Cleveland is a much older neighborhood. Also, the architecture of the houses in the North is different than in the South. This neighborhood is a lot older than the one where we lived in Florida."

An hour and a half into the tour, Michael announced that he was bored and wanted to head back to the house so that he and Kwame could go swimming in the pool Nigel had put up in the backyard. It was a hot summer day, and Tamara could see the appeal of spending it playing around in a pool rather than being cooped up in a car seeing the old sites.

"How about an ice-cream sundae before we head home?" Tamara asked. It was a rhetorical question, because the lure of the pool or not, she didn't expect the boys to pass up ice cream. As expected, both the boys answered with exuberant yeses to the idea of creating delicious sundaes.

Tamara giggled. "All right, ice cream it is." She drove to an old favorite ice-cream shop of hers in Fairfax that she had loved as a child, where it was made fresh daily. She was happy to see that the shop was still there.

Tamara parked, and they all headed inside, where the boys ordered sundaes loaded with chocolate and caramel sauces, gummy worms, chocolate chips and sugar sprinkles. It made Tamara cringe just to look at the sundaes. She opted for a simple scoop of butterscotch ice cream.

"So, what do you think of Cleveland?" Tamara asked once they were seated and eating their ice cream.

Michael swallowed his mouthful of food before answering. "It's all right so far," he said.

"You'll get used to it," Kwame told him. "And you'll love the winter, trust me. Making snowmen, having snowball fights… It's a lot of fun."

"I can't wait to see snow," Michael said.

Tamara looked at her son fondly, then at Kwame. The fact that he had Kwame here would make his transition a whole lot easier. She planned for them to attend the same school. Even if she got her own place, she would like for it to be in the same neighborhood where Callie and Nigel lived so that the boys could see each other often.

Finished with the ice cream, Tamara and the boys headed outside. They all piled into the car, but when Tamara turned the ignition, it didn't start.

She turned the ignition again, listened to the engine struggling, but again, it didn't turn.

Three more times told her that the effort was futile.

Tamara got out of her vehicle and groaned in frustration. The battery? She had known that she would need to replace it. She had AAA for assistance, but she also had jumper cables in her car.

The best option would be to try to find someone to help her get the car started.

"You boys stay here," Tamara said. Then she went back inside the ice-cream shop and asked if there was anyone who could offer up their car for a boost.

"I'll help you," said an older man who was seated near the door.

"Thank you," Tamara said as he followed her outside. "I knew the battery was on the fritz, but it's held up so far. I feel silly for not replacing it."

"It happens to all of us at one time or another," the man told her. "Which car is yours?"

"That one," she said, pointing to it.

"I've got the maroon Chevy Malibu. I'll drive it over and park it in front of yours."

While the man went the short distance to get his car, Tamara went to her trunk to get her jumper cables.

"Go ahead and pop your hood," the man told her once he parked and got out of his vehicle.

Tamara got behind the wheel of the car and did as he said. And then, out of habit, she put the key in the ignition and turned.

This time, the car roared to life.

"Oh," Tamara said, surprised. "That was weird." She got out of her vehicle and looked at the man, who smiled at her. "You didn't have the cables attached, did you?"

"No, not yet," the man said, smiling. "Looks like you didn't need me after all."

"No, I guess not. I'm so surprised it started."

"Maybe the battery is on its last leg, but not quite dead yet."

"Probably," Tamara concurred. "Thanks for helping me out. I'll take it to a mechanic as soon as I can."

"Have a good day, miss."

Tamara shook the man's hand before gathering up the cables and putting them back in her trunk.

Once Tamara was back in the car, Kwame said, "Aunt Tamara, Uncle Marshall can help you out if you need a new car. His family owns some car dealerships, so I'm sure you could get one from him."

Tamara's stomach fluttered at the mention of his name. Catching herself, she forced a smile. "I'm sure that won't be necessary. Once the battery is replaced, the car will be fine."

Tamara got the boys back home, and Michael and Kwame wasted no time getting changed into their swimming trunks. Tamara joined Callie on the back porch.

Tamara told Callie about the day, including the fact that her car had stalled.

"And then it just started on its own?" Callie asked.

"Yeah. It was weird. The battery is likely dying a slow death."

"You know, if you're in the market for a new car, Marshall can get you a deal."

Marshall, Marshall. Would she ever stop hearing his name?

"I'm not trying to play matchmaker," Callie went on when Tamara didn't speak. "But Marshall's got access to all kinds of cars and great deals, since that's his family's business."

Tamara inhaled a breath and then forced what she hoped appeared to be a nonchalant smile. "I get that. And if I need one, I'll talk to him. I'm pretty sure the issue is the battery, and once it's replaced, the car will be as good as new."

"Still, the car's getting up there. It's what, ten years old?"

"Yep. And I plan to drive it till it drops." She loved her Lincoln and wasn't keen on parting with it yet. It had been the first car she bought with the money she'd started earning as a real-estate agent.

"Okay," Callie said. "But if you want to look at something, let me know. We'll call Marshall. He can show you some options."

Tamara nodded. Then she said, "I have an idea I want to share with you. You might think it's crazy, but hear me out."

Callie took a sip from a tall glass of lemonade before asking, "What is it?"

Tamara suddenly felt a spate of nervousness. Not that she was embarrassed to share anything with Callie, but sharing her idea aloud was suddenly daunting. Was it a dream she could see to fruition?

"Tamara?" Callie prompted.

Tamara inhaled deeply before continuing. "Well, as you know, I always loved doing hair. You remember that I got my cosmetology license."

"And then you decided to get into real estate."

"Weird, I know. Doing hair was always a hobby of mine over the years. I guess you could say that it's my passion. But in Florida, I got involved in real estate, then selling time-shares, and I never pursued doing hair professionally. But now that I'm back in Cleveland, a part of my goal is to reshape my life. And part of doing that includes not wasting any more time doing work that just makes me money. I want to do the kind of work that excites me. The kind of job I'd do whether or not I was getting paid. Now, there's no doubt that I really loved my work in real estate, but if you asked me what my passion was, I would tell you that it's doing hair."

Callie nodded. "So what are you thinking of doing? Applying somewhere—"

"I think I want to buy a hair salon," Tamara blurted.

"What?" Callie's eyes widened in surprise.

"I know, it sounds totally crazy. Maybe I'm not planning to buy one yet, but I think I want to find a place to rent, see what I can do. But my heart is definitely telling me to open my own business."

"Are you serious?" Callie asked.

"Yeah." Tamara nodded. "After the year I had with Patrick, I really want to do something for me. I feel like it's important to not waste any more time."

"But you've never had a business before," Callie said, the voice of reason. "Obviously, real estate is a business in its own right. But it's not a storefront where you have to pay a monthly lease, hire staff."

"There's a first time for everything. Other people do it. Why can't I?"

"I get that. And I'm not going to try to discourage you. But why not go around to different salons and see if someone will take you on? Give you a chair to work out of, so you can build a clientele."

"No. I want to go big or go home, as they say. It's just become clear to me—I'm back in Cleveland, and this is where I grew up. And it feels like the right place to plant roots for Michael's sake. I always loved it here, though I can imagine I'll miss the warm weather when winter rolls around."

"Yes, you definitely will."

"But we'll adjust. And Michael has always talked about wanting to experience winter—kids love that. I'm sure he'll fare better than I will." Tamara grinned. "Callie, I know it seems hasty, but my heart is telling me to go for my dream. No matter how hard it is."

"Well, if that's what you really want to do..."

"It is. I spent my life doing what was safer. What brought me a guaranteed income. And I'm grateful for that. I don't have any financial concerns because I have a nest egg built up. That's going to allow me to play a little bit. See if I can make my dream come true. And if I can't, I can do what you suggest. Or go back into real estate." Tamara shrugged. "But I have to try, Callie. If I don't try, how will I know?"

"Then I support you." Callie sipped her lemonade. "Whatever you need from me, just tell me. I'll do what I can to help."

"Thanks, Callie. One of these days, I would like to head out and see some properties, get a look at what's available. Maybe you could come with me and help me search?"

"I'd be happy to. Just say when."

Tamara looked out at her son and Kwame splashing around in the pool. Nerves tickled her stomach at the thought of restarting her life here, but she could do it. "I'd love to have my business plans under way before Michael starts school in the next several weeks. That way, he can feel settled. And so can I."

"So you're really planning to stick around."

Tamara nodded. "It feels like the right decision. At least for now. I can always change my mind."

If things worked out as she hoped, Tamara would open her salon and also find a place for her and Michael to live. A place of their own. She couldn't stay with Nigel and Callie indefinitely. For the time being, the arrangement was fine. It would give her time to spend with her friends and relax a little. Forget about the chaos her life had been in Florida.

Michael climbed out of the pool and bounded toward the side of the house. "Slow down, son," Tamara told him.

"Okay!" But he barely broke his stride.

Shaking her head ruefully, Tamara got to her feet. "I'm going to get a glass of that lemonade. It looks good."

She went into the house, found a tall glass and then got the pitcher from the fridge. As she was pouring her glass, she could hear Michael's voice through the open kitchen window that was over the side of the house.

"...like being a detective?" Michael was asking.

"Yeah," Nigel said. "I love it."

Tamara leaned closer to the window, angling her ear to hear better. "Do you catch a lot of bad guys?" Michael asked next.

"I'm proud to say that I do," Nigel answered.

"Bad guys like my dad," Michael said, his voice sounding sad.

"Hey, buddy." There was a brief pause. "Whatever happened with your dad, you know that's not your fault, right? Your father is responsible for his own actions, and you're responsible for yours. You're a good kid—you didn't deserve that. But always remember that your mother loves you very much, and you'll be just fine."

"I hate him," Michael said. "I wish he wasn't my dad."

"That's understandable," Nigel said. He sounded sympathetic, not judgmental. "He hurt you. And hurt your mom. That's a lot to deal with for anybody, but especially for a kid."

There was another pause, and this time it lingered. Tamara

looked out the window and saw that Michael and Nigel were walking back toward the backyard. Nigel had his hand draped around Michael's shoulders.

Her eyes misted, and she blinked to keep the tears from falling. Her heart ached for her son, but there was nothing she could do but continue to give him love.

With her lemonade in hand, Tamara headed back out to the deck in time to see Michael heading onto the grass with a football, where Kwame was already waiting for him.

Tamara put her glass on the patio table and descended the steps. She approached Nigel, who was taking a position on the grass to play catch with the boys.

"Nigel," Tamara called, and he turned to face her. "Thank you," she said in a quiet voice as she reached him. "I heard what you said to Michael, and I appreciate it."

"No problem. He's a great kid, and I know he's been through a tough time. I just hope he can separate himself from his father."

"I hope so, too."

"I think you're doing the right thing by being here, in a totally different place. So far, Michael seems to be having a blast here. Kwame is familiar—they're already friends. I think that being here will be good for his healing."

"That was my thinking process," Tamara said. She planted her hands on her hips as she watched Kwame and Michael throw the football back and forth.

"Hey, over here!"

At the sound of the voice, both Tamara and Nigel looked over their shoulders. And there was Marshall, jogging into the backyard with his hands poised to catch the football. He wasn't dressed for playing any sport, not in stylish black slacks and a short-sleeved white shirt. Dang, the man looked as if he had just come from a photo shoot for Armani or some other top designer.

Michael threw the football as hard as he could, and Marshall sprinted to catch it. He extended his long, muscular frame with ease, palmed the ball and pulled it to his chest.

The boys cheered. Tamara crossed her arms over her chest. What was he doing here?

Grinning, Marshall jogged over to Tamara and Nigel with the ball. "Hey, Nigel. Hello, Tamara. Callie."

"Hello," Tamara responded, her voice a little clipped.

"Go deep, Nigel," Marshall told him, and Nigel took off toward the far end of the backyard. As Nigel neared the fence, Marshall threw the ball high and long. Nigel caught it and then held the ball up, triumphant.

"Boys and their toys," Callie called out.

Tamara made her way back up to the patio table. "Tell me about it."

Tamara sat with Callie, and they watched the men and boys play awhile longer. Watched them tousle and tackle and laugh.

A few minutes later, Callie pushed her chair back and stood. "I think I'll get the pitcher of lemonade. Looks like they can use it."

Tamara got to her feet. "I'll get some cups."

No sooner than they headed back outside, the boys ran toward the deck. Tamara began to pour the first cup of lemonade, which her son snapped up by the time she finished. Kwame eagerly took the second one.

Nigel wandered up to the deck, followed by Marshall. Tamara didn't make eye contact with Marshall as she poured but she then handed him the glass.

"I'll be out in a few minutes, Marshall," Nigel said. "I've just got to pack up my lunch."

Nigel headed into the house, and Callie followed him. Then Michael and Kwame bounded down the steps back onto the grass, leaving Tamara and Marshall alone on the deck.

At first, Tamara stared at the boys, saying nothing, still avoiding connecting eyes with Marshall. Because every time she looked at him, she felt a sense of unease that she didn't like.

But as the seconds ticked by, it seemed childish to avoid facing him.

So Tamara glanced at him and found him regarding her. Even with his dark sunglasses on, she could feel his eyes roaming over her face.

"So that's your son," Marshall said.

"Yep, that's my baby." Tamara smiled with pride. "Michael."

"He seems like a great kid."

"He is," Tamara concurred. Then she turned to the table, lifted her glass of lemonade and took a sip.

"The boys told me you had some car trouble today," Marshall said as she faced him again.

Brother. She wished they hadn't said anything. "I did," she said, steeling her back, "but it was nothing serious. The battery's giving me a bit of trouble, but I'll get a new one."

"You sure it's the battery?"

"I think so. Yeah, I'm pretty sure."

"If you want, I can take a look at your car."

"Jack-of-all-trades, are you?"

"Hmm?"

"You're a cop," Tamara said, counting that off on a finger. "Nigel also said you're a trained paramedic." She indicated a second finger. "Then there's the family business of selling cars. And you say you can also look at my car and figure out what's wrong?"

"With cars being the family business, as you say, it came naturally. My dad always knew his way around a car and taught me and my brother all about them, as well. So if you'd like me to take a look at your car, I'd be happy to."

It was a harmless offer, and yet Tamara had no intention of taking him up on it. "That won't be necessary. But thank you. I plan on getting something new by the fall anyway."

"You've got the Lincoln LS out front?"

"Yeah," Tamara said.

"Looks like it's about ten, eleven years old?"

"Ten."

"If you're planning to buy something new in the fall, you could always start looking now. I can take you around to some of my family's dealerships. Pretty much any car you want, I can find for you."

As if Tamara wanted to spend any more time with him than she already had! Even now, her pulse was racing faster than normal. "I'm good for now, thank you."

Marshall shrugged. "Suit yourself. But I'm here, if you need me."

Then Marshall leveled a charming smile on her before trotting over to the boys, and Tamara released a long, ragged breath. Thank goodness he was no longer beside her. She still felt hugely embarrassed about waking up in his house and not knowing whether or not she'd slept with him. She felt embarrassed by the conversation they'd had in the car, how she had rambled on about how their night together would be only a one-time thing.

Get over it, she told herself. She couldn't continue to feel tense around him forever. What had happened couldn't be changed, and embarrassment never killed anyone.

She just hated that he and Nigel were such good friends, because that undoubtedly meant that she would have to see him more than she cared to.

"All right, man," Nigel said, stepping onto the back deck. He was wearing a dress shirt, as Marshall was, and brown slacks. He carried a blazer on a hanger in one hand and a black thermal lunch bag in the other. "I'm ready, if you are."

Marshall said a goodbye to the boys before heading back over to the deck. "Callie, it's always nice to see you," Marshall told her. "Tamara, as I said, let me know if you need me."

Callie and Nigel exchanged a brief kiss, then Marshall and Nigel made their way around the side of the house toward the front.

Callie sidled up to Tamara, raising her eyebrows as she looked at her. "If you need him, huh?"

Tamara gave her friend a sidelong glance. "That's not what

he meant. He was offering me assistance if I wanted to buy a new car."

"Mmm-hmm," Callie countered, a lopsided grin dancing on her lips.

Chapter 7

Tamara was on Marshall's mind the entire drive to the station with Nigel. Did she really have such a dim view of him? Yes, she'd given him that whole spiel in his car about how he had hurt her cousin, but he hadn't quite been prepared for her apparent disinterest when he'd gotten to the house.

She had barely paid him any mind and spoke to him only because he'd made conversation with her.

Nigel had warned him that she was vulnerable, and the reality that she could be a lot like Lisa had convinced him to stay away. But seeing her again had sparked a renewed interest on his part.

She was beautiful, that much was obvious. But there was more to the attraction than that for him. Every time he looked at her, something happened between them. Something flashed in her eyes the first moment she looked at him. Then those beautiful brown eyes would widen, and her back would stiffen, indicating that she was uncomfortable in his presence. Marshall's gut told him that discomfort had everything to do with sexual attraction.

Maybe he was delusional—or maybe it was simply wishful thinking—but he couldn't help giving significance to what had happened the day of the wedding. Initially she had flirted with him on the dance floor. And then that kiss… You just didn't go from warm, playful flirtation to stone-cold when you didn't care one iota.

"Marshall?"

At the sound of Nigel calling his name, he faced him. "Sorry. You were saying something?"

"I was. But it seems that only your body is in this car with me."

Nigel was right about that. Marshall's mind was several miles away, back at Nigel's house… "What were you saying, man?"

"I was asking about Tamara."

Marshall felt an odd sensation pass over him at the mention of her name. "What about her?"

"I noticed… Actually, I'm not sure what I noticed between the two of you today. A weird sort of tension, maybe?" Nigel raised an eyebrow. "You sure nothing happened when she stayed at your place?"

"Definitely," Marshall told him, stressing the word. "Absolutely nothing happened. She was passed out, remember—and I wouldn't do that. Besides, you told me about what she went through. I wasn't about to make a play for someone in a fragile state of mind."

Nigel nodded. "All right. Good."

"I've got to say, however," Marshall went on, "she seems pretty strong to me."

"Yeah, sounds like she's had a solid year of therapy, so that's good. It's important."

"Really?" Marshall asked. Therapy was good. Therapy would keep her from making the kind of mistake Lisa had, he thought.

"Yep. From everything I gather, she's made great strides at

getting her life back on track. And now she's planning to make a fresh start with her life back here."

"So she'll be staying awhile?" That news pleased Marshall.

"That's the plan. At least for now."

"Good."

"Good?"

"Yeah. I mean, Florida must hold bad memories for her. I think it's great she's got the guts to leave and start over somewhere else. It shows strength."

"Definitely," Nigel agreed.

And maybe that strength even extended to other areas of her life—areas like dating. Maybe she was ready to put her bad marriage behind her once and for all.

At least, he hoped she was. And who could blame him? Marshall would have to be dead to not be physically attracted to her.

They got to the station, and no sooner than they went inside, they learned that they already had a new case. A shooting murder in Cleveland's west-side Cudell neighborhood.

"Never a dull moment," Nigel commented wryly. "Just let me get a coffee. Want one?"

"Sure. Grab me one for the road, thanks."

It was summer in Cleveland, and emotions ran hot. Marshall and Nigel still had two murders from the past week that they were following up leads on. Marshall had been hoping to work on those cases tonight. Now they would have to be put on the back burner as they investigated a fresh murder.

Ten minutes later, Marshall and Nigel arrived at the scene, a local park, where—given the early evening hour—it was a lucky thing that no children had been killed when the gunfire began. Uniformed police had already cordoned off the playground at large and the specific area where the victim had been killed. His body lay on the ground covered in a blanket to keep him from the view of the curious onlookers. The crowd was large, and people were watching with morbid fascination. Except for the group of weeping people, no doubt the victim's relatives.

Marshall would bet that the killing was drug related. Every day, he hoped people would learn. He hoped that the killing would stop. Drugs and guns didn't mix. But as long as drugs and guns were in the hands of people, his job would never be done.

When they exited their plain cruiser, they walked over to the body, wanting to assess the crime scene before they spoke to witnesses.

Someone in the crowd was bemoaning the influence of drugs in the community, practically preaching about how drug crime was taking the neighborhood's youth.

"Time to take stock of the witnesses," Marshall said, surveying the large crowd. "How about I work the people on this side of the road, you work the other side?"

"Sure," Nigel agreed.

Marshall approached the crowd, keenly watching for who made eye contact with him and who didn't. He was also searching for the faces of those who were already known to police, so that if need be, he could contact them at a later time and question them.

Marshall set about asking who saw what, knowing before he opened his mouth that the task would be futile. In a group as large as this, people didn't want to be seen talking about a crime as serious as murder.

Marshall worked the crowd to the best of his ability. handing out his business cards to everyone, imploring them to call if they thought of something. He knew that the call would come later, if at all. A witness with a conscience would only feel safe talking about the crime without prying eyes and ears.

"Anything?" Marshall asked Nigel when they met up again.

"Nobody saw nothin'…. You know how it goes."

"Yep." And then, as Marshall looked out at the crowd at large, he locked eyes with a young woman. Maybe twenty years old. She held his gaze for a long beat, and then she turned and began to rush away.

The victim's girlfriend? A witness?

All Marshall could hope was that she had his or Nigel's card, and that she would be in touch soon.

Tamara spent the next few days looking through the classifieds in the paper as well as online for possible locations for her salon. She wanted to do a preliminary search to get an idea of what was out there before getting in touch with the real-estate agent she'd spoken with the week before she'd left Florida. As someone in the business, she knew her way around listings and what to look for. This way, when she spoke to the agent, she would be able to make suggestions, and they could both work as a team.

On Thursday morning—after weighing the pros and cons of her plans to open a salon—Tamara got her cell phone and found the number she had stored for the agent she had contacted from Florida. Then she pressed the icon to dial the number.

"Victoria Doxator," came the friendly female voice.

"Hello, Victoria. This is Tamara Jackson. We spoke a few weeks ago. I'm the one from Florida. I called you about the property—"

"On Clark Avenue. Yes, I remember. But I'm sorry—that salon is gone."

"That's okay," Tamara said. "You might remember that I told you I'd be heading to Cleveland? Well, I'm here now."

"Great. So I take it you're ready to start looking at some properties?"

Tamara's stomach tightened with anxiety. She wanted to do this, but there was also a sense of fear. It wasn't easy to pursue a goal that was radically different than what you had done before. She was most definitely stepping out of her comfort zone.

"I am," Tamara said. "Did you get a chance to find some locations for me?"

"Yes, I found several that you might like. When are you available?"

"What's your schedule like?" Tamara asked. "It's Thursday. I can meet you tomorrow, if you have the time."

"Ooh, tomorrow won't work. I'm booked solid. I believe I've got some time on Monday. Just let me open my schedule." A few seconds later, she said, "I have a two-hour slot open on Monday, if that works for you. That gives me time to call and arrange for the viewings. I'd like to take you around to as many locations as I can."

"That would be great," Tamara said. She wandered over to the bedroom window, which faced the backyard. "I also saw some properties online. I can email you my list, but I'm sure there'll be some crossover."

"Definitely. Will Monday work? One o'clock?"

Pushing the curtains aside, Tamara saw Michael and Kwame kicking a soccer ball. She eased her butt onto the window ledge. "One o'clock sounds great."

"We can meet at my office and from there go and see all the options."

Tamara watched the boys playing. And then her stomach lurched painfully when she saw Marshall round the corner into the backyard, followed by Nigel.

Again? Her heart pounded. He was here again?

And good Lord, could he look sexier? He was wearing denim jeans that hugged his powerful thighs and a cream-colored shirt that was unbuttoned to his midchest, giving Tamara a tantalizing glimpse of those muscular pecs and hard abs.

"Hello? Hello?"

Tamara finally registered that Victoria was speaking to her. "Oh, um. I couldn't hear you for a moment," Tamara lied. "Must have been the connection. What were you saying?"

"I was asking if you would prefer that I email or text you the address for my office?"

"Oh, you can text me." Tamara felt frazzled. "The number you have is for my smartphone, so I can easily look the address up on the GPS if need be."

"These smartphones are so amazing," Victoria said. "Where would we be without them?"

"Mmm-hmm," Tamara agreed, thinking that the view outside her window was also pretty amazing. She slipped off the ledge and pulled the curtains closed far enough that she could secretly peer through them without being seen.

"So, one o'clock," Tamara said. "I'll be there."

"Excellent," Victoria said, sounding extremely chipper. "I'll see you then."

"See you then," Tamara echoed. Then she ended the call and continued to look through the crack in the curtains. Marshall and Nigel were now near the deck. Marshall was facing her direction as he spoke to Nigel, one leg raised on a step.

Tamara knew it was hot outside, but did he always go around in a shirt unbuttoned practically to his navel?

Suddenly, he looked toward her window. His eyes seemed to lock on hers, and Tamara swallowed. Surely he couldn't see her, could he?

He continued chatting with Nigel, and she assumed he hadn't seen her. Then the two of them started walking toward the right end of the backyard, which would take them past her window in a matter of seconds.

Tamara quickly took a step backward, her eyes following his every movement. And right when he was in front of her window, Marshall looked at it, and again, it seemed that he was looking directly at her.

And then he grinned.

Tamara jumped back even farther, her heart racing. He *had* seen her. If he hadn't, he certainly wouldn't have smiled!

Oh, God.

Her heart continued to beat irregularly. She didn't want Marshall thinking that she had been secretly checking him out.

Yet, after several seconds had passed, she crept back to the window. Carefully tried to look outside.

She couldn't see Marshall or Nigel. Only the boys.

Taking a breath, she shook her head, disappointed with herself. What was her problem? So what if Marshall was incredibly hot? He wasn't her type.

And even if he was, she wasn't interested in dating.

But I suppose if you ever wanted...a little something...Mar-shall would be very good at...that. Callie's words sounded in Tamara's mind. And much to her dismay, a wave of heat passed over her.

"Time to take a shower," Tamara said to herself.

A cold one. To banish any more thoughts like that from her mind.

Chapter 8

A few days later, Tamara realized that there would be no escaping Marshall. Not only had he invaded her dreams in a shockingly sexy way since she had seen him in the backyard on Thursday, but she learned he was coming over for Sunday dinner.

"Marshall's having dinner with us?" Tamara asked, a sense of alarm causing her stomach to tighten.

"Mmm-hmm." Callie was at the sink washing potatoes for baking. "He typically comes over on Sundays. Besides, he and Nigel have to talk about some plans for an upcoming event the police station is hosting in partnership with the Big Brothers association."

Tamara folded her arms over her chest and nodded. "I see." Why was she so bothered by the fact that Marshall was going to be here? Her discomfort was irrational, and she knew it.

"You got a problem with him coming over?" Callie asked, casting a sidelong glance in her direction.

"No. Of course not. I was just…just wondering, is all."

* * *

An hour and a half later, the cookout on the patio was complete, and everyone had eaten their fill of the delicious steaks that Nigel had grilled.

The boys were playing on the grass, music was playing and the adults were enjoying conversation. Mostly Marshall and Nigel were regaling the women with crazy stories of the events that happened while on the job.

As the laughter over the story about an elderly shop owner who had attacked an intruder subsided, Marshall gazed at Tamara, an easy smile on those sexy lips of his. And Tamara understood in that moment why he bothered her so. It was that easy charm and command of his sexuality, as though a mere look from him at whomever he desired and the woman would be his.

"I'm heading inside for a beer," Marshall announced as he stood. "Can I get any of you something to drink?"

Nigel lifted his beer can and shook his head. Callie, who sat beside Nigel with her arm looped through his, said, "I'm good, Marshall."

Marshall stood before her. "What about you, Tamara?" She wasn't certain if there was a twinkle in his eyes, and maybe she was being sensitive thinking he was having a bit of fun at her expense. He had to have remembered how she behaved the first night with alcohol, and surely it couldn't have escaped him that she had only lemonade over dinner.

"No," she said, trying to keep emotion from her voice. "Nothing for me."

"Can I get you anything else?"

Tamara looked up at his oh-so-fine body. Then she swallowed as an unwanted thought flitted into her mind.

The thought that she wanted a taste of *him.*

Good grief, what was wrong with her? It had been that long, she supposed, since any man had really shown an interest in her. Much less one so fine.

Much to her dismay, she wasn't immune to him.

"I'm perfectly fine," she told him and was happy when he disappeared inside the house.

But all too soon, he was back outside, and this time, he took a seat beside her. "So, how's the car?"

"It's still running well right now, thanks for asking."

"Come with me." As quickly as he'd taken a seat, he stood and offered her his hand.

Tamara looked uneasily at him, then caught Callie's eye, who was looking at her with curiosity.

"Um…" Tamara hedged.

"I need to show you something," Marshall told her.

"Show me something?" Tamara asked. "What could you have to show me?"

"Relax," Marshall said with an easy grin. "It's out front."

Tamara again looked at Callie, who had an approving grin on her face. Then she looked back at Marshall, wondering what he was up to.

"Come on," Marshall said, his hand still extended.

Tamara took his hand, and he pulled her to a standing position. Then he started with her down the steps toward the grass.

"Just showing her something, Nigel," Marshall said over his shoulder, and Tamara turned to see Nigel looking confused and Callie giving her two thumbs up.

"Are you really that afraid of me?" Marshall asked when they rounded the corner to the side of the house.

"Of course not." Tamara pulled her hand free. "Just curious."

"It's a surprise."

He had a surprise for her?

Tamara's eyes narrowed as she followed him to the front of the house. Was this a ploy to get her alone? "What could you possibly have to show me out here?"

In answer to her question, she heard the beeping of car doors opening. "This." Marshall beamed at her, then walked toward the Ford Edge parked on the street. "This car is from one of my parents' dealerships," he explained. "It's a year old, with low mileage. It was one of the demo vehicles—"

"You brought a car?"

"To see if you like it. Like I was saying, the mileage is low, and the price is great. Because you're a friend of mine, the price can be lowered."

"Marshall, I thought I told you that I didn't need a car."

"Yes, that's what you said. But your car is getting up there in age, so it doesn't hurt to explore the options. Might be the time to trade that in and then get into a new vehicle. It's a crossover SUV, so bigger than a sedan, but not overwhelming."

Tamara shook her head. "I tell you one thing, and you go and do what you like anyway. I don't want to be pressured to buy a car."

"This isn't pressure."

"Isn't it?" Tamara challenged.

"No. That's why I brought it to you. So you can check it out *without* pressure."

Tamara harrumphed. "I can't believe you would even pretend to know what I might like."

"If you don't like it, that's fine. I was just trying to be helpful. Figured we could take this for a test drive."

Tamara looked at the car, then back at Marshall. It was white and looked sharp. "This really wasn't necessary."

"Does that mean you don't want to take it for a test drive?"

He was smiling at her as he asked the question. She didn't know anyone who had a perpetual smile on their face, and she wanted to distrust him for that reason alone. She knew his smile had charmed many, and she didn't want to become the next notch on his belt.

She wanted to tell him no, that she wasn't going to get in the car. The time she spent in the car with him coming from his place the morning after the wedding had been almost too much for her to bear. Being in close quarters with him again was not advisable.

"Let me ask you this," Marshall began. "If someone else brought you this car for you to test drive, would you make a big deal about it? If Nigel had taken you to a dealership and said he could get you a better price, would you get upset?"

The question needed no answering. Of course she wouldn't get upset. She was being testy because Marshall had done it, because she had no clue what his ulterior motives might be.

"It's obvious you have a hard time taking no for an answer," Tamara finally said. "I told you I was happy with my car. But fine. We can go for a test drive. Even though I'm not ready to buy anything else."

Marshall walked toward the car, and when he got to the sidewalk, he extended the keys to her. "You go ahead and drive. Would you like me to come along with you, or does that thought scare you too much?"

Tamara's eyes widened. "Scare me?"

"Obviously you have some objection to me as a person. Because of your cousin? Heck, that was years ago. I keep telling myself that you couldn't possibly be holding that against me now."

Tamara's lips parted but she said nothing.

"So I figure there's got to be another reason. If you're uncomfortable around me because of what happened with your ex, I understand that. I get it. But I can't help wondering if it's something else." Marshall's voice rose on what sounded like a hopeful note.

Tamara glanced away, unable to meet his gaze. "Of course I'm not afraid of you. I have no reason to fear you. I might not be as trusting as I was in the past, but I don't look at all men as evil." Of course he didn't scare her in the sense that Patrick had.

If anything, she was nervous that he would seduce her…

At the thought, she felt a flush of heat and again wondered what was wrong with her. A solid year without the touch of a man and she had somehow lost her senses.

Tamara drew in a deep breath and hoped that Marshall didn't notice her concerted effort to calm herself. She was acting silly. Priggish, really. And there was no need for it. Marshall was being nice, thinking of her. He had proved himself to be a decent guy, even if he was a womanizer, and she needed to stop acting as though he was out to get her.

"Sure you can come along with me," she said. "It's just… I'm not making any promises. Like I said, I'm not really ready for a new car quite yet. I typically like to run my cars until the day they give up the ghost." She smiled. "But please, I'd like you to show me everything about this vehicle."

Marshall went around to the driver's-side door and opened it for her. She got behind the wheel. "Here are the levers to adjust your seat," he told her, gesturing to the bottom of the seat beside her legs. His hands skimmed her thigh as he reached past her, and though she knew it wasn't deliberate, she felt a little tingle nonetheless.

Oh, yes, it was quite clear that she was attracted to Marshall on a physical level. She could pout and avoid eye contact with him and act as though everything he said or did offended her, but the truth was she was fighting a fierce attraction.

As he went around to the other side of the car, Tamara adjusted the seat until she felt it was right for her. She looked through the rearview mirror and adjusted that, as well.

"This is the console," Marshall said. "There's XM radio, a GPS." He went over several features of the car. "This is a fully loaded model, and it's a great. And as I said, I can get you an even deeper discount. Basically cost to the dealership."

"That's very generous," Tamara said graciously.

Then she turned the key over in the ignition, and the Ford hummed to life. A quick check to see that all of her mirrors were in position, and she started off.

Tamara drove through the neighborhood, taking the car below the speed limit on all of the smaller side streets. "Let's take it on the main road," Marshall told her after five minutes. "That's the only way to really get a feel for the vehicle."

So she did. She took the car out onto the main strip. At first, she was still cautious, staying below the speed limit. She fiddled with the stereo, finding an old-school hip-hop station on the XM dial. TLC's "Ain't 2 Proud 2 Beg" filled the car.

"Oh, yeah," Marshall said, easing back in his seat. "Old school. TLC."

Of course, it would have to be *that* song.

"So how do you like it?" Marshall asked.

"It rides real smooth." Until now, Tamara had convinced herself that she didn't need a new car. But she couldn't deny that this one came with a lot more bells and whistles than her older Lincoln. "I like it a lot."

"You can see others," Marshall said. "Like I told you, no pressure. If you want to see a Lincoln or a Lexus…anything… let me know."

Tamara nodded.

About ten minutes later, Tamara was heading back to the house. They were both listening to the music and not saying much, which suited her fine.

Then, just as she was about to make the left onto the street that led to Callie and Nigel's, Marshall placed a hand on hers and said, "Pull the car over."

Tamara looked at him. "Why?"

"Because I'd like to talk."

She narrowed her eyes. "We have been talking."

"Not really."

Tamara met his gaze again, not knowing if she should make the left turn or head through the stop sign and pull to the right. "Marshall, what is—"

"Just pull over."

Tamara swallowed, unsure. Then, seeing that a car was driving up behind her, she hit the gas, went through the stop sign, pulled the car over to the curb and put it into Park.

"You know what I hate?" he began. "I hate that when you look at me, you don't really make eye contact. It's like you see me, but you don't really want to see me."

Tamara made a face. "What?"

"Are you going to deny that there's a wall between us?"

A few moments passed. Tamara had no clue what to say.

Finally, she made a sound of derision and said, "You're imagining things."

"Then why is it that even now, you won't directly meet my eyes?"

Tamara sighed softly and then looked into his eyes. And as she did, she felt a rush of heat.

It was the very reason she had avoided looking at him.

Marshall's lips curled in a smile. "Yes. There you go. Finally some real eye contact."

"Can we go now?"

"You know, what happened with your cousin was a long time ago. I'm really a nice guy."

"I think others might beg to differ. Others besides Gloria."

"So you're judging me solely based on the opinions of others? And from years ago at that?"

"Marshall, this is silly."

"Is it?"

"Of course it is. You want me to look you in the eye? To prove what?"

In an instant, he had his seat belt undone. "To prove that I'm not crazy."

"Huh?"

"To prove that what I'm feeling isn't one-sided."

Tamara's eyes widened as he leaned forward. Her back stiffened as he gently placed a hand on her face. What was he—

"I admit. Maybe I wanted you to pull the car over before we got to the house so that I'd have an excuse to do this."

Tamara had been so startled by Marshall's actions that she'd tensed, expecting him to plant his lips on hers in a forceful kiss. Instead, his fingers were gently stroking her skin, and he was staring into her eyes as though he aimed to weaken all of her defenses with the power of his gaze.

"You have beautiful eyes," he said, his voice a whisper. "I like when you look at me. You shouldn't be afraid of what you see."

Tamara was mesmerized by his touch. She was like a deer

caught in the headlights, unable to move, even though the danger was imminent.

Marshall brought his free hand to the other side of her face, and then he was gently framing both of her cheeks. Her heart began to pound furiously as he ever so slowly edged his mouth toward hers.

Tamara had only time to sigh in protest, the question screaming in her mind: *What are you doing?* But she couldn't form words.

Then his lips were on hers. They were as soft as they looked and moved over hers with a surprising gentleness, as if he were taking his time to get to know her. But the rush was just as sensual as the kind that came from a full-blown kiss.

Marshall's tongue flicked over her bottom lip, then the top one, before seeking entrance to her mouth.

Tamara's lips parted as if of their own volition. Then Marshall's tongue delved into her mouth, sweeping across the breadth of her own tongue. His fingers trilled her skin along her jaw and her neck, adding to the sensations flowing through her. It was a slow, hot kiss, and she was left panting.

Just as she surrendered to the sweet sensations and gripped his shirt with both of her hands to hold on for the ride, Marshall pulled back. Startled, Tamara looked into his eyes, wondering why he was doing this to her. She saw a smile on his face, a twinkle in his eyes.

And she immediately felt embarrassed for losing control with him.

"This is a game?" she asked. Before he could even speak, she continued. "Yes, of course it is. You kissed me because I kissed you the night of the wedding. And you wanted—"

He kissed her again, smothering her words. Tamara mewled against his lips, a sound mixed with protest and desire.

This time, when he pulled back, his eyes searched hers.

"I kissed you because I wanted to share one where we both meant it. No games, no fronting. Just a kiss between two people who are attracted to each other." He paused. "I meant it, and I'm pretty sure you did, too."

She did. And she wanted more.

That was what scared her.

Tamara turned forward in her seat, heat emanating off of her body in waves. She put the car into Drive and started off, making a U-turn, not daring to look at Marshall beside her.

Less than a minute later, she was back at the house. She parked the car and hopped out, before he could even say anything to her. She started for the front door, jogging up the steps without even looking back at Marshall.

When she went into the house, she saw Callie. "Where were you?" her friend asked.

"Um, Marshall brought a car here he thought that I might be interested in. He wanted me to take it for a test drive."

"And are you?" Callie asked. "Interested in the car?"

The door opened again, and Tamara looked over her shoulder at Marshall as he entered the house. At the man who had just warmed her entire body with that scintillating kiss.

She turned back to Callie. "No. I'm not interested. Definitely not."

Chapter 9

The next day, Tamara exited her car in a rush about ten minutes after one. Again, her vehicle had given her trouble starting, which didn't make sense because she'd had a brand-new battery installed.

By the time Tamara was closing her door, she saw the smiling woman approaching her with her hand outstretched.

"Tamara?" she asked.

"Yes." She took the offered hand.

"I'm Victoria Doxator." Victoria pumped her hand with a strong grip. "It's so nice to finally meet you."

"Very nice to meet you, as well." Tamara felt flustered. She didn't like being late. "I'm so sorry I'm late. I had a bit of car trouble."

"Oh, no."

"It's nothing serious," Tamara said.

"Oh, good." Victoria turned toward a gold-colored Lexus SUV. "This is my vehicle. The first location isn't far from here."

Five minutes later, Victoria was parking the car in front a

building with a for-lease sign in the window. "This is the first location," she said as they exited the vehicle. "I think it's a great choice, but as I said, I have others to show you, so you don't have to decide right now."

Tamara nodded. She studied the exterior of the salon. It was a little small, but that wasn't necessarily a bad thing. She didn't want to bite off more than she could chew with a huge salon that she couldn't keep filled.

Moments later, she followed Victoria into the property and looked around eagerly. It was dusty and had the musty smell of a place that hadn't been used in a while.

"The building is solid," Victoria explained. "This only needs cosmetic work. Fresh paint will make the place look brand-new."

Being in real estate, Tamara was able to look past what was to see what a place could be. "Are the chairs and dryers staying?"

"Yes. Everything you see here is staying."

It had only the main fixtures like chairs and hair dryers, but the accessories, like carts, were missing.

"As we discussed, the rental term for this location is one year."

Tamara nodded as she surveyed the place, trying to imagine how she would put her touch on it. She liked it. The chairs were a bit older in terms of style but in good condition from what she could see.

"What about the neighborhood?" Tamara asked. "I noticed some other unoccupied businesses here, so that's a concern." A good location was key. Foot traffic would be beneficial for her.

"Definitely—some of the businesses here have suffered because of the recession," Victoria said. "But that's reflected in the price for this property. The neighborhood's rebounding, though. Slowly, but surely."

"It has promise," Tamara said. "But I would definitely like to see the other locations."

"No problem. The second location is just a couple blocks away."

The next location was way too big for Tamara's liking. As was the price. It was the kind of salon that was meant to have several stylists. It was more modern and certainly beautiful, and she would love to have a salon like that one day. But she couldn't start off this grand.

They went to two more locations, and the fourth one, in the neighborhood of Cleveland Heights, piqued Tamara's interest. It was about the size of the first location, but looking through the window, Tamara could see that it was more contemporary.

Victoria unlocked the door and led the way inside. "Now, as you can see, this one is in a busier location. For that reason, the lease is a little higher than the first location I showed you. Also, this one is a bit bigger."

It was deeper, for sure. "And it definitely looks to be in better condition. It doesn't have that musty smell."

"Right."

Tamara looked around eagerly. And as she did, she had that fluttery feeling in her gut that told her this was the one. It was bright, with lots of light flowing into the store from the windows. Like the second salon they'd looked at, this one had newer equipment. The chairs were more modern, and the decor was elegant. Tamara could easily see that there would be minimal work to get this place into the shape she wanted. A few small touches like paintings on the wall, and this place would look great.

"I like this one," Tamara said.

"Oh, good. I don't think it will last, to be honest. It went up on the market only a couple of weeks ago. And the lease can start as soon as you'd like."

"The location is great, and there's room to grow," she went on, thinking that perhaps one day she would add a stylist to the shop. She nodded enthusiastically. "Yes, this is the one that I like. Let's get the paperwork started."

Victoria beamed. "Excellent. Like the other locations, this one requires a year lease."

"Perfect."

"You wouldn't have to do much to this place before you could open for business," Victoria went on. "Which, from what you've said, is ideal."

"It is. I like the size, the fixtures, the fact that this looks like a turnkey operation. I can basically get the lease, then open for business."

"You're certain?" Victoria asked.

"Yes. Definitely. Let's get the deal started. And if we can negotiate the price a little, that will be fantastic."

Victoria shook her hand. "I'll get you the best deal possible."

Tamara did a slow turn in the salon, and a smile tugged at her lips. Her own salon. Her dream coming true.

Tamara went back to Victoria's office to deal with the paperwork, and she felt a huge level of satisfaction as she signed her name on the offer to lease the property.

Then she went to her car in the parking lot, and it failed to start yet again. She then wondered if something worse wasn't wrong with the car.

She remembered Marshall's words, that it was better to trade the car in now than later. Maybe he was right.

Tamara called Callie. It was the only thing she could do.

She expected her friend would pick her up, but she couldn't have been more surprised when, fifteen minutes later, Marshall's black BMW pulled up alongside hers in the parking lot.

He rolled down his window, and Tamara did the same. She looked at him in confusion. "Marshall?"

"I was at Nigel's when you called. I told Callie that I'd come pick you up, and take a look at the car in the process."

Tamara felt a tickling sensation in her stomach and the urge to smile. She was happy to see him.

Marshall got out of his car, and Tamara followed suit. As he sauntered to the front of her car, he said, "Pop the hood."

"Oh, right." Tamara went back into her vehicle and pressed the lever to release the hood latch.

Marshall raised and secured the hood, then looked down at the engine. Tamara went to stand beside him, watching him curiously.

"Same problem today?" he asked. "It just wouldn't start?"

"I put the key in the ignition, and it made a sound like it would start, but it never did. I replaced the battery, so I have no clue what's wrong."

"Yeah, I see." Then he leaned forward and began examining different parts of the engine. Lifting wires and touching other things that were foreign to Tamara.

"Do you see the problem?" she asked.

"Not immediately." He dusted his hands off, but the grime from the engine remained. "Try starting the car for me."

Tamara went into the car and did as he asked. Again, the car tried to start, but didn't.

"I think it's the starter," he announced from behind the hood.

Tamara went to his side again. "The starter?"

"That's my best guess, looking at everything in here. Obviously, I don't have the machine to run a diagnostic test here, but based on how the engine sounded, and that we can rule out the battery, I'm thinking it's the starter."

"So, you *do* know your way around cars," Tamara said. "That must have been a skill that came in handy."

"Sure. It's great to be able to diagnose the problems with my own car. And friends'."

"Only then? What about when you have a female friend over and you don't want her to leave?" Tamara asked, her tone playful.

Though she had been joking, Marshall gave her a serious look. "I've never had to disable a car or do any other trick in order to make a woman stay the night."

"I wasn't necessarily saying you used it as a ploy…"

"Oh, were you trying to suggest that I would disable a woman's

car so she would spend the evening in my house baking cook-
ies with me?"

"Actually, I was trying to be funny. Sorry if it didn't come
out that way."

Marshall took a step toward her. "I think you were digging
for information. Probably trying to figure out if the rumors
you'd heard were true."

Tamara's eyes widened as he took yet another step toward
her.

"Like I told you yesterday, I don't play games. If I like someone, I just let her know." His eyes were holding hers steadily,
and Tamara swallowed. "And I like you, Tamara. God only
knows why, since you seem desperate to write me off as a
player."

"Let me... I've got wet wipes in the car."

Quickly, Tamara spun around and went to the car, where
she got the small package of wet wipes from the glove com-
partment. By the time she was standing and turning around,
Marshall was there.

She gasped in surprise. "I didn't expect you right behind
me." She drew in a calming breath. "Here." She opened the
package of wet wipes and offered one to Marshall. When he
didn't take it, she placed it in his hands.

His fingers quickly curled around hers, and he pulled her
close. "Marshall—"

He drowned out her protest with his lips, in a kiss that was
immediately deep and passionate. The kind of kiss that set her
body on fire and made her crave more.

He broke the kiss and brought his lips to her ear. "Anything
you want to know about me," he said softly, "all you need to
do is ask."

Tamara felt a shiver of desire. "Um. What I want to know
right now...is what do I do with my car?"

Marshall roared with laughter. The sound was infectious,
filling her with a sense of lightness. He possessed such an easygoing, stress-free quality that Tamara wanted a good dose of it.

"I do have to head to work, but I'll call for a tow for you. Then I'll take you back to the house."

His voice was low and sultry, and he may as well have been suggesting they go back to his place, given how her body reacted.

"All right." She folded her arms over her chest.

After they called for a tow, and Marshall called the station to explain he might be a few minutes late, Tamara was sitting in the front seat of the BMW.

"So what are you doing in the parking lot of a commercial Realtor?" Marshall asked. "Looking for work?"

"Actually, I'm planning to open a hair salon. No, I'm *going* to."

"Hair?" Marshall asked. "Didn't Nigel say you were in real estate in Florida?"

"I was. And I know this seems like a completely crazy leap, but I got my cosmetology license years ago. In fact, I kept up with various courses over the years—despite my husband not seeing the point. That way, I could do my friends' hair or my own." She shrugged. "I guess…maybe in my subconscious I always knew that one day, I'd end up trying my hand in this field of work."

"And here you are."

Tamara smiled. "I went to see some places today, and I'm making an offer on one."

"Wow. You mean business."

"Yeah, I do. My ex-husband never supported this dream, which is why I never tried to pursue it seriously. I kept it as a hobby. But I've learned not to waste time in life."

"I couldn't agree more," Marshall agreed. "Life is too short."

His eyes held hers, and Tamara got the sense that he was referring to her. Her body tingled, and she knew that if she were at Marshall's house, she could easily be tempted.

She quickly looked forward, trying to jar the thought from her mind. "So." She cleared her throat. "Tell me about this event you and Nigel are working on. And why is it over the Fourth of July weekend?"

"Ah, our community-outreach event. It's in the west side's Cudell neighborhood, which is very high risk. Lots of drugs. Too many murders. That's the area where Nigel and I work out of, and sadly we're always busy." Marshall paused. "Why the Fourth of July weekend? As cops, we know that when holidays come around, there's often an increase in crime. More people get together, and you think it should be festive—and it is— but people also have more time on their hands. There's more alcohol, tempers flare. More gun crime. You get the idea. Our station has been doing this event for a few years now, and the aim is to keep the young, at-risk boys off the street. We do it in partnership with the Big Brothers association, and we try to pair up the boys with big brothers who can be in their lives and be a positive influence. Also, the kids get to hang out with cops and realize that we're not the bad guys. We're out there to help. But that, yes, there are negative consequences for your actions if you don't do the right thing. Being able to spend the day with the cops helps them to realize that we're not out to get them. We want to help them."

Tamara smiled at Marshall. "I'm impressed."

"Impressed that I would be involved with the event?" Marshall asked, narrowing his eyes in question. "Or impressed with the process in general?"

"To be honest…" Tamara inhaled deeply before speaking, then decided to just say what was on her mind. "I didn't think that would be your kind of thing, but again I don't really know you."

"Exactly. You don't really know me. You know the guy you *think* I was years ago."

"Sorry" was all she could say. But perhaps, for her, it was easier to think of him as a player. That way, she would have a reason to keep the walls up where he was concerned.

"When are you going to take some time to get to know the real me?" Marshall asked.

"I am getting to know you now," Tamara said.

"I mean like on a date. Not sitting in the front of a car waiting for a tow truck to arrive."

"A date?" Tamara echoed, chuckling nervously.

"By now you ought to know that I don't bite. Unless…" His words trailed off, and his eyebrows rose, the implication clear.

Tamara's face flushed. For a moment, she couldn't speak. Because she was suddenly envisioning Marshall's teeth on her neck…

Boldly, she said, "You want to get me into bed? And you say you're not a player."

"*Player.* There's that word again." But Marshall was smiling, as though nothing fazed him. He had an easy answer and warm attitude even when she was gently snubbing him.

"I'm attracted to you. I'm not going to lie. But my attraction extends beyond simply hoping to get you into bed."

"And therein lies our conflict. I'm not interested in pursuing a relationship."

Marshall pursed his lips as he looked at her. "Maybe you're interested in something else…?" One of his eyebrows rose, his expression hopeful.

"And there you go again."

Tamara turned away, but Marshall placed a finger on her chin and urged her to look at him again. And once again, he brought his mouth down on hers, kissing her deeply. His fingers slipped into her hair, pressing against her scalp as he held her in place almost desperately. Tamara gripped his wrists and kissed him back with equal fervor, done with the pretense that she didn't want him.

If they were at his house, they would end up in his bed. And she would welcome it.

Marshall was one sexy specimen of a man. His look alone sparked heat along her skin.

He was awakening her femininity in a major way.

There was a knock on the car window, and both of them

jumped apart. Tamara whipped her head around, embarrassed to be caught making out in a car like a teenager.

Marshall grinned at her. "Looks like your tow is here."

Tamara didn't respond, her breathing too ragged. All she could do was watch Marshall exit the car.

And wonder what it was about him that made her so fiercely crave sex.

Chapter 10

Since he had arranged for Tamara's car to be towed to the Ford dealership owned by his parents, Marshall had her number. And though he had been at work for hours, he'd spent much of his time trying to think of a reason to call her. A reason to send her a text.

When he'd offered to arrange a loaner car for her, she had refused. He'd then suggested bringing her to a couple of his parents' dealerships tomorrow, and she refused. Anything else he offered by way of help, he was certain she would turn down.

The truth was, he simply wanted to see her. Any excuse would do. He wanted to kiss her again, feel the moment she surrendered to him.

An hour before the end of his shift, he sent her a text telling her that he was thinking of her. Honest. No fronting about wanting to help her as an excuse to see her.

But Marshall got no response.

The next morning, however, he was surprised when he saw her number flashing on the screen of his phone.

"Hello?" he said.

"Morning," she said softly. "Did you have a chance to check on the car?"

"I'm expecting a call from Service when they have a diagnosis."

"Oh. Right." Pause.

"Is there something else on your mind?" Marshall asked.

"I...I don't want to be any bother, but you had mentioned being able to get me a loaner car?"

"It's no bother at all," Marshall said. "I can swing by and pick you up in twenty minutes."

"Okay." She sounded nervous. Hesitant. "That'll be good. Thanks."

"No problem. See you shortly."

Tamara was nervous as she awaited Marshall's arrival. She hadn't been able to put the kiss they'd shared out of her mind all night—or his text. He was wooing her, and she was warming to the idea of seeing what could happen between them.

Or maybe—though the very thought surprised her—she was simply ready to scratch an itch that needed to be scratched.

That wasn't so wrong, was it? To have female needs? She quickly dismissed her thoughts and got dressed. She put on a pink skirt that came to above her knees and a white blouse with a frilly collar. She applied mascara to brighten her eyes and a gloss to make her lips pop.

"Wow, you look pretty," Callie said to her when she went to sit in the living room.

"Oh, really?"

"Why are you all dressed up?"

"Marshall's coming by. He's taking me to get a loaner car."

"Ahhh." Callie's tone said she totally understood.

"You don't mind?" Tamara asked. "If I leave Michael here?"

"No, of course not."

"You're going out, Mom?" Michael asked from the kitchen table, where he was sitting with Kwame.

"I'm going to look at some cars. I think it's time to get a new one."

"Oh, can I come?" Michael's eyes widened with excitement.

"It's going to take a while, and you'll be bored. You'll have more fun here with Kwame. Trust me."

"Aww."

"I'm going to take you boys to the park," Callie said. "And if you want, I can even take you to a big pool with a waterslide…"

"Yay!" both of the boys exclaimed in unison.

The doorbell rang. Tamara's heart pounded against her chest.

Callie scooted off to the door. "Hey, Marshall," she greeted him in a singsong tone.

He hugged her. "Morning, Callie."

"I understand you're taking Tamara car shopping?" Callie looked over her shoulder at her, a smile dancing on her lips. For whatever reason, Callie appeared to love the idea of Tamara spending more time with Marshall.

"Yep." Marshall met her gaze. "Hey."

Tamara walked over to him. "You ready?"

"If you are."

"I am. All right. Let's go. See you later, Michael and Kwame. Have fun." She hugged Callie briefly. "Thank you for watching Michael."

Callie waved a dismissive hand. "Of course."

Then Marshall said his goodbyes, and they both headed to his car.

Neither spoke until they were well down the street and away from the house. Marshall turned to her, saying, "You look nice."

"Thank you. So do you." And he smelled incredible. Whatever aftershave he was wearing made him all the more scrumptious.

"Thank you." He paused. "You know, I was thinking—I've got three cars. I can lend you one of them. It'll save you having to go to the dealership and bother with waiting for a loaner."

"Oh." Tamara's breath caught in her throat. "So we'd go to your house?"

"The cars are in my garage, yes."

Tamara drew in a shaky breath. Then she said, "Well, if you're happy to loan me a car, I'll borrow it. For the time being. Until I get mine back. Or until I get a new one or whatever."

She closed her eyes and tightly shut her lips. Why was she so nervous?

"I've got a Buick Enclave, but that might be a little big for your liking. I also have a sporty Audi." He nodded. "Yeah, I think you might like that. But you'll decide when we get there."

Tamara stared at the large, sprawling colonial-style homes as Marshall turned onto a cul-de-sac. The first time she had been here, she hadn't paid particular attention to the homes because she had barely been able to think of anything other than the thought that she had slept with him. Now, she took in the perfectly manicured lawns, pruned hedges and circular driveways.

Marshall pulled into the semicircular driveway lined with hedges. He had a beautiful home, no doubt about it, but it was the kind of house that was typically filled with married couples and two-point-five children.

"Not exactly your typical bachelor pad," Tamara couldn't help commenting.

Marshall put the car in Park and turned to her. "No," he said in a low voice, "I guess not."

He held her gaze for a beat before exiting the car, and then he trotted around to the passenger side and was opening the door for her just when she finished unbuckling herself. Marshall offered her a hand.

Tamara paused before accepting it, and once she did, he pulled her out of the vehicle. But he didn't release her hand as he walked to the front door. And she didn't try to pull it away.

He opened the door, and only when they stepped inside

did he let go. But only to turn to face her and slip his arms around her waist.

Tamara drew in a sharp breath. From the moment she'd gotten into his car to head to his house, she had known that the visit would be about more than simply loaning her a car.

"Welcome to my home…again," Marshall said with a hint of amusement in his voice.

Tamara fully expected him to kiss her, but he didn't. He pulled his hands from around her waist and took her hand in his for a second time. "This, on the right, is my dining room. It seats twenty."

"It's beautiful." She had glimpsed it the first time she was here but hadn't explored the room in her haste to escape Marshall's house. "That's black walnut, right?"

"Mmm-hmm."

He headed toward the left, into the great room. "This is my great room. I like to unwind here after work, watch a movie or put on some music. I've got lots of room, and I like to entertain. I typically have a Super Bowl party here."

"With a television like that, it's no wonder."

He took her into the kitchen, and when Tamara saw it, she actually sighed in delight. It was a dream kitchen. It was large, with black-granite countertops and maple cabinetry. The center island was the perfect place to prepare food, or even to put out buffet-style dishes during get-togethers.

"I *love* this kitchen," she told him.

"You like to cook?"

"I love to. I'm not gourmet by any means…but this kind of kitchen could inspire me to be."

Marshall drew her to him. "Is that so?"

She hadn't meant to sound as if she were planning to become a part of his life, and she didn't have time to correct him before his lips softly came down on hers. The kiss began slowly. He trailed one hand lightly down her arm, his touch electrifying her skin. Then Marshall deepened the kiss, and his other hand went to her neck, skimming her skin with delicious tenderness as his tongue swept over hers.

She was breathless when he pulled away from her. Breathless as she looked up into his eyes that were heated with desire.

Then he continued. "And off the kitchen is a deck, where I have a Jacuzzi. But what I really want to show you right now is the bedroom."

It had been a long time since Tamara had made love, and she was both nervous and excited. Nervous that with a man like Marshall, she might fall short of his expectations.

He nuzzled his nose against hers as he brought his fingertips to the area above her breasts. "Can I show you the bedroom?"

Tamara's chest was heaving. "Yes," she rasped, and then she initiated a kiss, looping her arms around his neck.

Marshall made a gruff sound of desire, then put both hands on her waist and pulled her body against his. She could feel the rock-hard evidence of his yearning for her.

And it turned her on even more.

He tore his lips from hers, took her hand in his and, without a word, led her to a staircase that started to the far right of the kitchen. He hurried up the steps, and she followed close behind. Then he whisked her down the hallway and through an open door, pulling her into his arms and planting his mouth on hers the moment they crossed the threshold.

"Oh, baby," he said, moving his lips from her mouth to her neck. He kissed a path along her skin from the base of her neck to her ear. Tamara gripped his shoulders and moaned.

His mouth went to the other side of her neck, and this time, he added flicks of his tongue. A shiver of desire went through her entire body like a shock wave.

He began to kiss her lips again, and as he did, he walked with her toward his bed. Their tongues mating, he began to undo the buttons of her blouse. The task complete, he eased back and looked at her.

Marshall made a sound of pleasure as he took in the sight of her breasts clad in a lacy white bra. It was the kind of bra that pushed her breasts up and made them look full and luscious.

"You're so beautiful." He trailed a finger across her chest, over her bosom.

Tamara made a soft mewling sound as he brought his mouth down onto one mound and kissed it softly before doing the same to the next one. He left her bra on and went back to kissing her, something he did with incredible skill.

Though it had been a long time, Tamara eased her hands beneath Marshall's shirt. She wanted to tease and tantalize him, too. His skin was warm, and she felt his body quiver at her touch. She moved her hands higher, slowly, enjoying the feel of the hard grooves and planes of his washboard abs.

She grabbed at his shirt next, pushing it upward. Understanding what she wanted, Marshall pulled back and raised his arms. He was much taller than her five-foot-six frame, and she couldn't pull the shirt completely off of his body. He took over and tossed it to the floor.

Then he nudged her shirt off of her shoulders, and it landed in a heap on the floor next to his shirt. He looked at her bra, determined that the clasp was at the back, and he gently spun her around. As his hands worked the clasp, he reached his mouth around to kiss her from behind…and an erotic charge shot through Tamara's body.

Marshall unclasped her bra, and with his lips still on hers, he removed it from her shoulders and down her arms. As he let it fall to the floor, he cupped both of her breasts. He kneaded them, ran his hands over them and grazed her nipples with his palms.

Tamara broke the kiss as she began to whimper. Marshall continued to play with her nipples, which were extremely sensitive, and kiss her shoulder blades at the same time.

The sensations assaulting her body were overpowering. Her sweet spot was moist, and she was desperate to make love to him.

"Marshall…"

"Yes, baby," he said, then spun her around and urged her onto the bed. Once she was on her back, he stretched out beside her. He met her gaze, pulling his bottom lip between his teeth as he looked at her. Then his eyes ventured lower, to her breasts. He indulged in the sight of them for several seconds before finally leaning forward and taking a nipple into his mouth.

"Ohhh." A long breath oozed out of Tamara. The sensation was incredible. He suckled her nipple slowly, exquisitely. He trilled it with his tongue. He drew it deep into his mouth. And Tamara thought she might climax from the pleasure of it.

"You like that?" he asked softly.

"Yes." Her voice was faint.

He moved his mouth to her other breast, where he tortured her with pleasure. This time he used his finger to brush over it while teasing her with his tongue, intensifying her pleasure.

Tamara tossed her head back and forth as her body writhed. "Oh, my goodness."

He continued his loving assault and slid a hand beneath her skirt. It trailed up her thighs until he found her center. He stroked her through her panties before urgently slipping his fingers beneath the fabric so that he could touch her feminine core. She arched her back as he used the pad of his thumb to massage her most sensitive spot, all the while using his tongue to pleasure her breasts.

The sensations were divine, and she allowed herself to indulge in something she hadn't had in way too long. Her head began to grow light. She knew she was close to losing all control....

She opened her eyes, caught sight of his mouth moving over her nipple, and an erotic rush shot through her. She began to climax, arching her back and gripping the sheets as a wave of pleasure washed over her.

She rode that wave, enjoying all of its intensity, and Marshall continued to please her until every bit of the orgasm drained from her. Then he kissed her again, deeply, before getting up from the bed and removing his pants.

Tamara watched him, sucking in a gasp when she saw him drop his briefs. My goodness, he was large and hard. He was a beautifully sculpted man, and a part of her couldn't believe she was sharing his bed.

He went back to her, found the button and zipper on her skirt and made fast work of freeing her body from it. Then he pulled her underwear off, and they were both completely naked.

Some of her strength regained, Tamara got up onto her knees as Marshall joined her on the bed. She immediately brought her lips to his chest and began to kiss his skin. Slipping her hands around to his back, she dug her fingertips into his flesh and was rewarded when he groaned in pleasure.

She kissed. She nibbled. She trailed her tongue over his perfect body. And then she brought one of her hands around to stroke his shaft.

He growled in response, then took her by the shoulders and spun her onto her back. Swiftly, he spread her legs, settled between her thighs and began to gently enter her.

Tamara cried out from the pleasure. He took his time, gliding into her slowly so that there would be no discomfort. And when he completely filled her, she gripped his shoulders and moaned long and hard.

"Yes, baby," he whispered hotly into her ear. "Oh, you feel so good."

His thrusts were slow at first, his moans deep as he savored the feelings. Then the two of them began to move against each other with more ease, picking up speed. Soon, their movements were hurried and their sounds of pleasure unabashed.

Tamara tightened her legs around his buttocks as she sensed he was nearing his own climax. She moved with him, grinding hard, their passion explosive.

She began to feel the arms of rapture grip her again, and just as another orgasm claimed her, Marshall thrust into her hard and growled as he, too, was caught up in the euphoria.

Moments later, their bodies hot and slick, Marshall kissed her. It was a tender, lingering kiss.

The kind of kiss that made Tamara think she wanted much more of what she'd just had.

Chapter 11

Tamara spent far too much time at Marshall's house. They rested in each other's arms for about thirty minutes and then made love a second time. Round two was more energetic than the first, and they experimented with different positions.

Afterward, Tamara showered, because the last thing she wanted to do was head back to Nigel and Callie's place smelling like sex.

She was glad that she'd pulled her shoulder-length hair into a ponytail before she'd left with Marshall, because now all she needed to do was freshen it up. Callie would never notice that anything was amiss.

"I spoke with Service at the dealership," Marshall said when she came out of the shower, dressed. "The problem is definitely your starter. The job will run probably close to a thousand, so do you want them to go ahead and fix it?"

Tamara considered. She'd already replaced the battery. Now the starter. What else might go wrong if she hung on to the car? She didn't want to spend more, especially when she knew she was planning to replace the car sooner rather than later.

"You still think they'll take my car as a trade?" Tamara asked.

"You can trade it in, no problem. You'll get a fair price."

"Then tell them to hold off on doing the work. Maybe tomorrow or the next day we can get together and I can see what's available at a good price? The Ford Edge is nice, but I'd like to see what else is out there."

"Of course. And I'll be happy to take you around."

Tamara was happy to find the house empty when she returned, with Marshall's Audi as her temporary car. She'd been gone a long time and didn't want any questions or curious speculation from Callie. It wasn't that she couldn't tell her friend what had happened, but Tamara had done something she hadn't expected, and she wasn't quite ready to share it with anyone else yet.

Tamara checked her messages and saw that she had missed a call from Victoria, so she returned her call.

"Victoria Doxator."

"Hello, Victoria. It's Tamara Jackson."

"Hi, Tamara. I have good news for you. Your offer has been accepted!"

"Oh, my goodness. Wow."

"Yep. Occupancy July fifteenth. How does that sound?"

"It sounds like I've just become a business owner." Her stomach tingled with nerves. "And I'm going to have a lot of planning to do before then."

"Congratulations."

"Thank you."

"We can go over the paperwork tomorrow, before the holiday. Or we can wait until next week."

Tamara bit down on her bottom lip. "I've got to find a lawyer. Yes, why don't we set something up for next week."

No sooner than Tamara had set up an appointment for Tuesday, Callie entered the house with the boys. "Hey!" Callie greeted her.

"Hi, Callie." She rushed over to Michael, who was wearing his swimming trunks and had a towel slung around his neck. She wrapped her arms around him. "Hello, son. Did you have a good day?"

"It was *awesome!* That waterslide was wicked."

Tamara chuckled. "Was it, now?"

"Mmm-hmm," Kwame concurred.

"Okay, boys. Time to get into dry clothes."

They ran off toward the bedroom, and Callie approached Tamara with her hands on her hips. "Isn't that Marshall's Audi out there?"

"Yeah. He said that he was more than happy to lend me one of his cars, since he's got a few."

"Interesting."

"Not so interesting," Tamara countered. "He just wanted to be helpful. Tomorrow, he'll take me around to look at new and pre-owned cars."

"Hmm." Callie's voice was full of delightful suspicion.

"What?"

"To think that you rejected the idea when I suggested Marshall could help you get a new vehicle."

"I know. Let's just say I've seen the light." Tamara could hardly hold back a little smile. She had seen the light all right. She had seen the sun, the moon and stars as she experienced the utmost pleasure in Marshall's arms.

But she didn't want to tell Callie about that. Not yet. She had no clue where this thing with Marshall would even lead. For now, she had scratched an itch and she felt amazingly better for it.

"And I have some other news," Tamara said. "I heard from the real-estate agent. My offer for the salon has been accepted!"

Callie's eyes widened with surprise and happiness. She reached to hug her. "Girl, I am so proud of you! I can't believe you are doing it. Carving out your own way in the world. That's excellent."

"I almost can't believe I'm doing it, either. But it was the right spot. A cute little salon, already in great shape. The area in Cleveland Heights is perfect. I think that I'll get a lot of business there."

"I can't wait to see it," Callie said. "And as you know, I'll do anything to help. In fact, I think we should plan for a big party. With Natalie's fundraising and event-planning history and with Deanna being a music star, we can throw one heck of a launch party for you. There's no doubt we can get great media coverage. Help put your salon on the map right from the get-go."

"Yes!" Tamara was getting even more excited. Much of the planning she wanted to do on her own, but she realized that Callie's family had the kind of resources that could only boost her business. "That would be fantastic. A catered event at the salon and unveiling to the media…"

"When Deanna gets back from her honeymoon, I'll run the idea by her. I'm sure she'll be happy to help. And we can talk to Natalie about it anytime. She can start to get the ball rolling with some ideas."

"Thank you. Callie, you have been a godsend. I'm happy that you've opened your home to me, and you're giving me the time I need to get my business together."

"You're my best friend. Of course you're welcome here. And you're welcome for as long as you want."

"I know." Tamara had no doubt that Callie would never kick her out. But part of Tamara's plan to carve out her future included finding a place for her and Michael to live. She couldn't rely on Callie and Nigel's kindness forever. "I just want you to know that I appreciate you."

"I love you like a sister. Never forget that."

Tamara's eyes began to mist. Things were coming together for her. She was truly putting the ugly past behind her.

She had even gotten lucky.

Not that she expected that to lead to anything, nor did she want it to. But it was another step in the direction of healing, getting over the past once and for all.

* * *

Over the next few days, Tamara went car searching with Marshall and settled on a Chevrolet Equinox. It was a year old, with low mileage, and Marshall was able to get it for her at cost. She put her offer in just before business closed for the Fourth of July holiday and was sent to pick up the car the following week.

Tamara had also hung out with Callie and her sister Natalie and some of their female friends, who were making plans about what to cook and bake for the ADOPT-A-SON community-outreach program. There was a lot of talk about how well anticipated the event was, and how important it was for the leaders in the community to step up and show the younger boys that they cared.

"So many of these boys don't have a father figure," a friend of Callie's was saying. "Being able to spend the day with cops and other men in the community really has a positive effect on them. Sometimes, these boys have fathers who are imprisoned or dead. They're at risk of following the same negative path their own fathers took. That's why this event is so important."

The other women agreed, and they all were looking forward to helping out during the event. It was really about the men and the boys, but the women were going to be providing the food.

Until this moment, Tamara hadn't thought anything of the idea of having Michael participate. In fact, over the past few days he and Kwame had been quite excited about it. Kwame was proud to have a father who was involved, and Michael was looking forward to the experience of the games and other activities. But now, hearing what Callie's friend had said, Tamara was reconsidering.

"Earth to Tamara," Callie said.

Tamara's attention snapped to her friend. "Huh?"

"I was asking if you would make your famous cheesecake. I was telling the ladies that you make the best cheesecake I've ever tasted."

"Oh. Sure. I'll be happy to." But as the chatter went on,

happy and carefree, Tamara tapped Callie's arm and asked her to step aside with her.

Callie looked at her with concern once they were in the hallway, away from the other women. "What's wrong?"

"It's this event." Tamara paused, inhaled deeply. "All this time, I had no issue with having Michael attend. Now I wonder if it's the best thing for him. Maybe it's going to hit him—the fact that he doesn't have a father in his life anymore. He's been coping well so far, and I don't want to open the wound."

"Oh, sweetie." Callie rubbed her arm. "I understand that you are concerned. But the truth is, the emphasis doesn't seem to be on reminding the boys that they don't have a father in their lives, but on just being there for them and hanging out with them and letting them see that the life of the streets is not the best choice. Kwame's going to be there, and I'm sure Michael would have a good time if he goes."

Tamara nodded slowly. "I suppose you're right. I just...I just want to protect him from anything that might hurt him. But I know that the reality is he has to deal with what happened. And in order to deal with it, he's going to have to face the pain sometimes."

"And you are going to be there for him as he does." Callie smiled at her and then squeezed her hand in support. "We can't shield our kids from everything, but you're being a great mom. Never doubt that. He'll get through this with you by his side."

Tamara nodded, feeling better. She knew she couldn't protect Michael from every situation where he might be reminded that he didn't have his father present, and perhaps the weekend's events would be good for him.

"And you'll be able to keep an eye on him if you're there for the day working in the kitchen. Between all the hot dogs and burgers and ice cream we'll be serving, you'll be seeing Michael plenty."

"Yes, you're right." Tamara felt better about the idea already. She was still protective of Michael and wanted to be close to him. If he had some sort of meltdown seeing all of the other good fathers and thinking of his own who hadn't been too good, she could always comfort him.

"And if it makes you feel better, Nigel told me that Marshall said he would make sure to hang out with Michael for the day. Be a kind of surrogate dad to him."

Tamara's lips parted in surprise. "He did?"

"The same thought crossed his mind. With what has so recently happened with Michael's father, and the fact that Marshall has been getting to know him pretty well during his visits here, he figured it made sense that he pay special attention to him at the event."

Tamara was startled. And she wondered why Marshall hadn't said anything to her about his idea when they'd been out car shopping. Yet he had chosen to share this with Nigel instead.

"I hope you're not upset," Callie said, picking up on her mood. "As you know, he and Nigel are best friends. It's not like they were planning parenting strategies behind your back. Somehow, it came up, and they talked about it. I think it's a good idea. Michael's already familiar with Marshall. It makes sense."

Tamara crossed her arms over her chest, nodding, but still feeling slightly disturbed. She had shared her body with Marshall. Couldn't he have told her his thoughts about her son?

"When I first came here with Kwame," Callie went on, "he had no clue who his father was. My biggest fear was that he would be resentful, not accept Nigel as his dad when he learned the truth. But his reaction was exactly the opposite, and it's been wonderful. He was thrilled to meet his father, and my deception was forgiven. I know Michael can get through this, as well. Kids are extremely resilient."

Callie's words truly made Tamara feel better. "Yes, Kwame has dealt with it all just fine."

"The key is just to love them through everything." Callie smiled warmly. "And you already do that."

"Thank you," Tamara said. "You've made me feel better about tomorrow."

Callie slipped her arm around Tamara's waist and began to walk back toward the kitchen with her. "What are friends for?"

Chapter 12

The Cudell Recreation Center was loud with chatter and laughter. The kitchen was busy with women preparing the burgers and hot dogs for a lunch meal everyone would enjoy. The men and boys were hungry, and providing food for all of them was no easy task.

As luck would have it, it was raining, so the community center was filled to capacity. The basketball court was full, and the pool was active, as well. Everyone was hoping that the sun would come out by the afternoon so that some of the activities could be moved outside.

Though Tamara had been concerned that Michael would become overwhelmed with the reality that he didn't have a dad around anymore, the few times she had stolen glances at him, he was laughing. It did her heart good to see that he was enjoying himself.

"Michael has really taken to Marshall," Callie said as the two women headed out into the hall, where the tables and chairs were being set up for lunch. "He's been with him most of the day."

"Yes, I noticed." Passing the glass doors to the gym, Tamara spotted Marshall and Michael side-by-side on the basketball court. Seeing her, he waved. "He's truly come alive today," Tamara added with wonder. "He seems happier today than he's been since we got here."

"I noticed that, too," Callie commented.

Tamara watched Marshall and her son awhile longer, wondering if the same easy charm he had with women extended to everyone. Clearly, he was easy to relate to.

A short while later, when it was announced that lunch was ready, the men and boys charged into the dining hall. As she expected, Michael took a seat beside Marshall.

There was a light in his eyes that caused a bittersweet emotion to fill her heart. She was glad that he was happy. But the way he had taken to Marshall showed her just how much he missed having a father in his life, even though he had never once told her that.

Lord knew she wished she could have spared her son the trauma Patrick had put them through. He'd been thrown into the world of adult problems, when he should have been able to be a boy.

Tamara sighed softly as she watched Marshall rub Michael's head affectionately. While she appreciated Marshall spending time with her son, she wasn't exactly elated about the idea. Because she didn't want Michael seeing him as a surrogate father beyond today. She knew that he might. She and Marshall had slept together once, but they certainly weren't headed down the path of a relationship.

As the afternoon rolled around, everyone was thrilled when the rain stopped and the sun came out. Tamara went outside with some of the other women, passing out juice boxes and Popsicles. She watched Marshall and her son playing soccer with a group of boys and men on the field. She watched Michael get the ball. Watched him try to kick it to Marshall. They had certainly bonded. He had taken to him as if he were truly his dad.

Callie sidled up to her. "It's been a great day," she said. "A real success."

"It certainly has."

While most of the women had stayed out of the men's way, bringing them drinks and food but not engaging in chatter, Tamara couldn't help noticing that one of the younger volunteers always found a reason to talk to Marshall. The first couple of times she saw her lingering around him, she hadn't thought anything of it. The third time, her curiosity had been piqued. And now, as the soccer game progressed, the woman—who she had learned was named Heather—was on the edge of the field near where Marshall and Michael stood. She was cheering loudly, urging Marshall on.

Did he know her?

Tamara had an unsettling feeling in her stomach. Of course he knew her. Heather was in her mid-to-late twenties, stunning. A full head of wavy hair that flowed down to her midback. Many of the women who were volunteering today had put on minimal makeup, not come dressed to impress. Rather, they had come to work. But Heather was wearing four-inch platform heels, tight jeans and a low-cut top. Her eyelashes had a thick coat of mascara, and her lips stayed with a fresh coat of lipstick. She had come to this event to look cute.

Now Tamara couldn't help wondering if she had specifically come dressed like this for Marshall's benefit.

The hours passed, and things were beginning to wind down. Boys were heading home. It was the supper hour, and the snacks that remained would not suffice for everyone. But a handful of kids lingered.

Marshall, Michael, Nigel, Kwame and a handful of others were playing basketball on the outside court. And of course, that was where Heather was. On the sideline. Tamara had noticed her specifically go over to Marshall more than once and speak to him, and it had irked her. But more so, she had been irked with herself.

She had slept with Marshall knowing exactly what the deal

was—that it was simply a sexual thing. She had no right to feel even a smidgen of jealousy.

Tamara told herself it wasn't jealousy that had her calling Michael over when Heather was once again fawning all over Marshall. "Yeah, Mom?" Michael asked.

"We're leaving."

Michael's face dropped with disappointment. "But I'm not ready to leave," he complained.

"Michael," Tamara said, gently but firmly. "As you see, people are starting to go home."

"But why does it have to end so soon?" he complained.

"The event was scheduled to end at 6:30," Tamara said. "It's been a long day for everyone, and people have to go home."

He crossed his arms over his chest and sulked. "That's stupid."

Tamara blew out a harried breath, but bit her tongue. Michael wasn't usually like this, but she knew that he'd been through a hard time. This was the first bit of fun he'd had in a while, and clearly he didn't want it to be over.

"Michael, you need to watch your tone."

"Well, it is!"

"Are you forgetting that you also have to get up in the morning? You're going away with your aunt Callie and uncle Nigel and Kwame." Callie and Nigel had planned an overnight camping trip for the long weekend, from Sunday to Monday. It had been scheduled before Tamara got to town. They had invited her to come along, as they were simply renting a camper and going to an RV park. But Tamara had declined, saying that she would prefer to stay back and unwind. Enjoy a little time to herself.

"It's not like I'm going to die if I don't get the most sleep in the world."

Her eyes widening, Tamara planted her hands on her hips. "Michael!"

Marshall, who had been occupied with Heather a few feet

away, came over when he heard Michael raising his voice. "Hey, bud," he said to him. "What's the matter?"

Michael glanced down. "This shouldn't be ending so soon."

"I hear you. It feels like it's only been a couple of hours, right?"

Michael nodded.

"The thing is, the community center needs to be cleaned up. The volunteers are itching to get home to their families."

Michael said nothing, just continued to look down.

"But…" At Marshall's words, Michael looked up expectantly. "Maybe if your mom doesn't mind, we can watch a movie back at Nigel's place. He's got that great home theater—it'll be just like going to the movies."

"That's a great idea!" Michael exclaimed, beaming.

"Did I hear my name?" Nigel asked, wandering over to them.

"Michael isn't ready for the day of fun to end, so I suggested maybe we can see a movie at your place."

"That's really not necessary," Tamara said. "It's a Saturday night. I'm sure you…have plans." Her gaze ventured beyond him to Heather, who was texting on her phone, but was making sure to linger close to Marshall.

Marshall followed her line of sight. "I've got no plans for tonight."

"Please, Uncle Nigel?" Michael asked. "Can we?"

Kwame, who had been a few feet away, also joined in the pleading. "Can we, Dad? Or maybe we can play the Xbox?"

"It's fine with me," Nigel said. "It just can't be that late of a night because we have to get up for our trip in the morning."

"Yes!" Michael exclaimed, pumping his fist.

"Marshall, you really don't have to," Tamara told him.

"I want to." His eyes held hers for a moment, but she looked away.

"All right, Marshall's coming over," Tamara said to her son. "Now go do your part and help clean up."

Michael ran off with Kwame, as if the idea of putting chairs away was the most thrilling one in the world.

Tamara stood there, not really regarding Marshall and expecting him to go back over to Heather, who was now looking in his direction. But he took a few steps closer to her.

"I think your friend is waiting for you," Tamara said and then mentally kicked herself. Why was she even saying anything that came off as jealous? She had no dibs on Marshall, nor did she want any.

"Who?" Marshall looked over his shoulder. "Heather?"

"It looks like she wants to talk to you." *Again,* Tamara thought silently.

"But I'm talking to you."

Tamara didn't react in any way, just crossed her arms over her chest and looked in Michael's direction. He was busily dragging chairs across the floor. "Wow. I can't believe him. Look at him being a little workhorse."

Marshall grinned at her. "He's excited that the day doesn't have to be over. I remember that feeling. You're having so much fun, you don't want it to end."

Tamara nodded. "I guess." She paused. "You were great with him today. He's really taken to you."

"He's a great kid," Marshall said. "I enjoyed hanging out with him."

"Thank you for putting a smile on his face. Honestly, I haven't seen him like this in a long time."

"No problem. That's what this day was all about. I'm glad he had a good time."

Tamara offered Marshall a smile as he looked down at her. The look lingered, and he smiled back, and warmth crept into her heart. She couldn't help seeing him in a different light. Obviously, he wasn't simply a shallow guy who spent his spare time chasing skirts. He was fun, caring and giving.

"Hopefully we have tired all the young people out, so they'll go home and go to bed. Instead of going out to linger on the streets at night."

"I hear that," Tamara said.

"Well, I'd better help clean up. See you back at Nigel's place."

"You really don't have to—"

"I want to," Marshall stressed. "In fact, why don't you head home and put your feet up? I'll bring Michael with me when we're finished here."

"Oh. No, that's okay."

Marshall narrowed his eyes as he regarded her. "You've been on your feet all day. And I'm pretty sure I noticed you limping a little bit. So go home, put your feet up. Rest."

Tamara hesitated a beat. "I really don't think—"

"Police orders. Michael will be fine with me."

Tamara eyed Marshall. He continued to surprise her. Was he truly this caring? "But the other women—"

He smiled again. "As I said, police orders. They'll be fine without you."

Marshall was certainly right. Tamara was dying to put her feet up. She had an ankle that bothered her sometimes if she was on it for too long. "Let me just check with Michael."

But when she asked her son if he was okay heading back to the house with Marshall, Michael practically shooed her through the door.

Tamara headed over to Callie. "I think I should probably head home. My ankle's been bothering me. Marshall said he would bring Michael with him. I know you're helping to clean up, but would you mind cutting out a little bit early?" Tamara had come to the event in the same car with Callie and the boys.

"You think you can navigate your way back to the house? I can just let you take my car, and I'll hitch a ride with Nigel."

"I grew up here, remember?" Tamara said, looking at her friend with a twisted smile.

Callie laughed. "Well, you have your key."

"See you back at the house."

Tamara gathered the plates and baking pans she'd brought, then headed out. But not before sneaking one last peek at her son.

Now that Marshall was coming over, he was no longer sulking, but grinning and laughing as he did his part to clean up. Seeing her son happy—especially after all he'd endured—tugged at her heartstrings.

But as she was about to start out the door, she noticed Heather head over to Marshall.

And she couldn't help wondering if the reason he had seemed so nice and thoughtful in insisting that she head home and put her feet up was because he actually wanted her out of the way so that he could flirt with Heather without her around.

When everyone was back at the house, Nigel and Marshall went downstairs with the boys, and Tamara stayed upstairs with Callie. She helped to prepare the cooler of food that Nigel and Callie would bring on their trip.

"You sure you don't want to come with us?" Callie asked.

"No, but thank you for offering to take Michael. I think I could use a couple days of rest and relaxation."

"I know the feeling. And we're happy to have him join us."

It was just before ten when Nigel came upstairs with the boys, rounding them up to brush their teeth and get ready for bed. Tamara could hear their conversation from behind her open bedroom door, where she had retired with a book.

She lowered the book, listening. Obviously, Marshall would be leaving shortly. Callie and Nigel were definitely going to bed, as well, as they were getting up early for the trip.

Tamara debated heading out of her room to say goodbye to him. Thinking back on the day's events, which included the flirtatious Heather as well as the reality that Michael was becoming closer to Marshall than she particularly wanted, she decided that she wouldn't say goodbye. It was better that she keep things between them less complicated. Keeping him at bay would accomplish that.

The quiet knocking at her door caused Tamara's heart to flutter. Especially when she looked up and saw Marshall peering in.

"Sorry to intrude," Marshall said. "But your door was open."

"I guess you're leaving," she surmised.

"Yeah. And I wanted to say good-night."

Tamara didn't get up from the bed. "Good night. Thanks again for spending time with Michael today."

Marshall took a step into the room. He looked at her as though he were trying to figure her out.

Tamara's gaze flitted beyond him. She didn't want Nigel or Callie or even her son to pass by the room and get the wrong idea.

"I'm leaving in a moment," he said, picking up on her anxiety. "I was just thinking that maybe we could go for dinner tomorrow. Since you'll be here alone."

Tamara hesitated. Then she said, "With all due respect, I'll pass."

Marshall narrowed his eyes, looking confused. "You'll pass? Why?"

It was a good question, one she didn't entirely have the answer to. She had enjoyed her time in his bed, and he no doubt wanted more of that. He would understandably assume that she wanted more of that, too.

But Tamara thought it best to put a halt to anything more between them. Part of it was seeing the way Heather had flirted with him, and knowing that Marshall was the kind of man women chased. Getting further involved with him would add an element of drama to her life that she didn't need. She had loved seeing her son happy today and was touched by Marshall's interaction with him. But she didn't want him or any other man derailing her plans.

"Because," she started, then stopped. "Dinner means dating, and I already told you that I'm not here to build any sort of relationship."

"Why does it feel like we took three steps forward and now two steps back?"

"It shouldn't" was Tamara's simple reply.

Marshall couldn't have looked more puzzled. "What's going on here?"

"Hey, Marshall, are you sleeping over?"

At the sound of her son's voice, Tamara whipped her gaze to the door. Michael wore a hopeful expression on his face.

Tamara climbed out of bed and went over to Michael. She wrapped an arm around his shoulder. "Marshall was just leaving. He came to my room to say good-night. Now you say good-night to him, as well, and I'll tuck you in and say a prayer with you."

Michael lunged at Marshall, throwing his arms around his waist. "Good night. I wish you could come camping with us."

"Another time, bud," Marshall told him. "Good night."

"Good night, Marshall," Tamara said firmly.

"We'll talk later," he said to her.

Tamara headed out of the bedroom with her son, not looking over her shoulder. But she sensed Marshall's eyes on her, burning a hole in her back.

Chapter 13

Marshall felt as if he had been sucker punched. He and Tamara had made love, and he had believed that they'd crossed a major hurdle. Coupled with all of the time they had spent while car shopping, at the very least he thought she considered him a friend.

Yet she had undoubtedly erected a wall between the two of them again. He had offered her dinner, and she'd barely considered it. But it wasn't just that. It was the way she had looked at him.

Or rather, not looked at him. She was back to evading his gaze, and that annoyed him.

The next morning, he was still thinking about her. Had she been jealous of Heather? That didn't make any sense.

Marshall decided to try again with her. Take a gentle approach. He was cognizant of the fact that she might be wary about men, which was why he hadn't suggested last night that she come to his place today, but that they get together for dinner. To continue the task of getting to know each other. Because what he knew of her so far, he liked.

He sent her a text, saying that he would love to get together at some point. That maybe they could go down to the water or do something else that she might be interested in. Go for a run, play some sort of sport if that was what she liked. He left it open-ended, for her to decide.

Her response via text, half an hour later, was a simple No thanks.

No thanks? That was all she had to say? Obviously, it was a brush-off.

Considering Marshall couldn't get her off of his mind, let alone understand why she was suddenly pushing him away, he got into his car and headed to Nigel's place. If she suddenly wanted nothing to do with him, she could at least tell him why.

Marshall pulled into the driveway and parked behind his Audi. Then he looked at himself in his rearview mirror and smoothed his hand over his closely cropped hair before he headed to the door.

He rang the doorbell and then waited. Several seconds passed. He rang the doorbell again.

When he still got no response, Marshall opened the screen door and pounded on the wood. Finally, he heard Tamara ask from behind the door, "Who is it?"

"It's me. Marshall."

A beat passed. "Why are you here?"

"Why am I here?" Marshall repeated.

"Yes, why?"

"You're not going to open the door?"

"I don't like unexpected guests."

Either she was wound up tighter than a coil, or she was afraid at the idea of seeing him. He had already seen her naked. Already kissed and touched her in places and had her moaning his name. Why was she doing this?

"So now I'm an unexpected guest?"

"You should have told me that you were planning to come over."

"I would have—if you had talked to me." After a few moments passed, Marshall tried a different tactic, going for a bit of lighthearted humor. "I'm a police officer. Coming to check on you. Ma'am, can you open the door, please?"

Another beat passed, and the smile on Marshall's lips fell flat. Was Tamara even on the other side of the door anymore? Or had she left him standing there like a fool? Marshall had never had to fight this hard for a woman's attention before, especially not one he had made love to. "Tamara?"

When there was still no response, he placed his hands on his hips, stunned. Clearly, she *had* walked away. Unbelievable.

Slowly, Marshall turned. That was when he heard the door open.

He whirled around. Tamara stood behind the screen door, pulling the tie on a white robe tight enough to show the form of her hourglass figure. Her hair was damp, indicating she had just come out of the shower.

Marshall's eyes roamed over that body, to her bare feet with the hot red toenails. "I thought you were blowing me off."

"Sorry." She pressed her hands to the folds of the robe, ensuring there was no slippage. "I wasn't decent. I just came out of the shower."

Marshall merely nodded, because he knew that the words on the tip of his tongue would not be welcomed. Telling Tamara that he was certain her nude body was far from indecent was likely to get him slapped.

Instead, he said, "Ah, I see."

"So why are you here?" Tamara asked.

"I just came to check on you. You're here alone. You know."

"Worried I would be afraid of weird sounds?" she asked.

It amazed Marshall that Nigel had ever described Tamara as fragile. She was feisty. Definitely not fragile.

"I figured that with Nigel and Callie and the kids gone for the weekend, you might not mind some company."

"And I'm pretty certain that I told you twice that I'd be fine."

Marshall stared at her, utterly confused. Where was the

woman who had gripped him, shuddered beneath him, cried out his name and begged for more? What had happened to her?

But his pride got the better of him, so he said, "Okay." Then he turned and headed down the stairs. He was almost at his car when he decided to look over his shoulder. Tamara had already closed the door.

Perhaps it was the fact that she had so easily dismissed him, or the fact that she was acting as though she had never been affected by his touch, but Marshall marched back to the door and began to pound on it loudly. Moments later, Tamara swung it open and looked up at him, a hint of annoyance in her bright, brown eyes.

"I thought you were leaving," she said.

"You know," Marshall began, "I'm not sure why you're giving me the cold shoulder. I'm trying to be nice."

"Nice?" Tamara actually chuckled. "Oh, of course. You're just a regular knight in shining armor."

Marshall cocked his head sideways and narrowed his eyes. "What the heck is that supposed to mean?"

"You're trying to be nice? Just out of the goodness of your heart, right? Come on, Marshall. You know that your game play is to get me back in your bed."

"My *game play?*" Marshall gaped at her. That was what her sudden attitude change was about? She thought he was only interested in sex?

He wanted to throttle her. Either that, or kiss her senseless.

"Exactly what kind of game do you think I'm playing? You've been in my bed. And you liked it." He watched her eyes widen, as though shocked at his words. "I made no bones about the fact that I'm attracted to you. You, however, are the one who wants to play games. You kissed me first, remember? Then you gave me some line about how you were doing it as payback for your cousin. Why don't you just admit that you were attracted to me? That you kissed me because you wanted to? And that you liked it. And you liked what we did in my bed. But what—you feel guilty now? Is that why you're giving me the cold shoulder? Or is it because you want more and you're afraid to ask?"

Tamara glanced away and scoffed. But there was something to the fact that she couldn't meet his gaze. Something that made him feel his remark had hit home.

He took a step closer to her, and she took a step backward. "If you want more," he said softly, "all you have to do is ask."

"I never *wanted* sex with you in the first place. What happened at your house... It just happened. I'm not the first woman who shared your bed, and I know I won't be the last."

Marshall took another step, closing the door behind him. "Is that what this is about? You wanting to believe so badly that I'm a player?"

"I saw you with Heather."

Realization dawned. "Is that what this is about?" He couldn't stop the small smile from forming on his lips. "You're jealous?"

"Don't be ridiculous."

"You're the one who mentioned Heather's name. She's just a friend of mine."

"And you're allowed to have as many friends as you want."

"And by *friends* do you mean lovers?" Marshall gave her a pointed look.

"We made no commitments to each other. I'm not naive."

Marshall didn't know whether to be flattered at the idea of her being jealous or annoyed that she was making excuses to avoid him. "Here's what I think. You had a great time with me the other day. Sure, we've gone around looking at cars and other things, but I bet that you want more of what we shared just as much as I do. But you can't tell me that, because you think I'm some bad evil guy who sleeps with a different woman every day?"

"I'm not sure I've met a man with an ego as big as yours."

"Tell me I'm wrong." His eyes roamed over her body slowly, taking in every beautiful inch of her, robe and all. It was the kind of gaze that would have her understanding without doubt that he wanted her back in his bed. "Tell me you don't want me."

Her eyes widened in alarm as she looked up at him. "I don't have to tell you anything."

He grinned. "Which is as good as telling me I'm right."

"Oh, please."

But again, she looked away.

Marshall crossed his arms over his chest. "So you haven't thought about having sex with me again?"

"I had an itch. I scratched it. That's all."

Marshall couldn't help chuckling. "So it was no big deal?"

"People have sex all the time."

There was a part of him that wanted to take her in his arms and kiss her until she begged him to touch her in all the places that made her weak. She was downplaying what they had shared together, which had been pretty incredible. For a first time together, Marshall had been amazed at how they had connected. "So whether we do it again or not, no big deal to you?"

She gave a nonchalant shrug.

"Wow. So then you should be up for an Oscar award for your performance in my bed last week. The way you held me, begged for me to touch you, to kiss you, to give it to you like this and *oh, yes, baby, like that...*"

Tamara's face grew dark with embarrassment as his voice trailed off, and Marshall grinned. He knew he was right.

"You're wrong for that," Tamara said softly.

"Why? Because I'm also right?"

And before she could say a word, Marshall closed the distance between them, slipped his arms around her waist and pulled her against his body. She moaned immediately, a soft, inviting sound that said she wanted him just as much as he believed.

And damn if that moan wasn't his undoing. He wanted this woman in his bed. The clean, fresh scent of her, the fact that she was naked beneath her robe... "Tell me you don't want to make love to me again," he said, his words more a plea than a question.

Tamara's eyes met his. Held. And he felt her breath shudder between them.

That was when Marshall lowered his lips to hers.

He skimmed her mouth with his own. A wisp of a touch, but it stoked his fire. Next, he gave her a soft, lingering kiss, his full lips pressing against her sensuous ones. When he felt her exhalation of breath, his mouth then picked up speed. He suckled her bottom lip before slipping his tongue between her now-parted lips. Her hands slipped around his shoulders. He pulled her closer, deepening the kiss as he did.

And then it was as if fire consumed them both. Tamara dug her fingers into his shoulders, and Marshall's own hands ventured over her behind. He pulled her hips against his groin, allowing her to feel the evidence of his desire for her.

Then one hand went lower, to the hem of her short robe, and he began to trail his fingers up the back of her thigh.

He wanted her. He wanted this feisty, spunky woman. But he didn't want her here. Not in his friend's place.

Besides, he wanted her to own her feelings. He wanted her to willingly ask for what she wanted.

"I'm going to head back to my place now," he began. He saw the surprise in her eyes. "With my big bed. My Jacuzzi tub in the backyard surrounded by large trees so that no one can see. I would love for you to join me there—if you want me as much as I want you. That will mean that you have to get in the car and come to me—no more games." He knew that he could easily lead her to the bedroom now, but then she could avoid taking full responsibility. She could claim she had simply been caught up in the emotions of the moment.

He wanted to give her no reason for excuses.

"If you're interested, I guess I'll see you there."

"Marshall..."

He opened the door and stepped outside. "I'll be there. The question is, are you willing to admit what you want?"

Then he headed to his car and didn't look back.

* * *

Once Tamara saw that Marshall had driven out of the driveway, she clenched her fists and let out a squeal. It was a squeal of frustration. A squeal of carnal hunger.

She *did* want him. He had been kissing her, making her feel hot and bothered. So why hadn't he just taken her to a bedroom here? Heck, the floor? Anywhere where she could satisfy her obvious lust for him.

But no, he had left the house. Left her body thrumming with extreme need. He'd made it clear that if she wanted him, she was going to have to go after him.

Tamara stood there, her back against the wall near the door, her chest heaving as her heart beat rapidly. She wanted to go after him; there was no doubt about that. But another part of her also wanted to stay where she was. She wanted to show him that he didn't have her all figured out.

The bigger part of her wondered why she craved him so. She'd had one taste of him, and it was as though she were now addicted. It was like a child having her first taste of candy and wanting more.

As much as she wanted to stay away to prove a point, she wanted another taste of him even more. So she got dressed. She put on a thong and matching bra and a dress that was easy to take off. Then she got into the Audi and headed to Marshall's place.

When she arrived and knocked at the door, it opened only a mere second later.

Marshall looked down at her and smiled. And then he asked, "What took you so long?"

Chapter 14

Tamara walked into the house. Marshall closed the door behind her. Then they immediately came together in a flurry of passion. Her hands squeezing and stroking his muscles. His hands groping her behind and pulling her against his groin. His mouth finding and claiming hers. Their tongues tangling with each other's, the kiss so desperate it was as if they both needed it to survive.

Marshall urged Tamara's behind upward, and she lifted one leg up around his hip. He pulled her up then, and she brought her other leg around his waist, locking both behind his back. As Marshall carried her like that up the stairs, Tamara looped her arms around his neck, holding on tight.

His mouth ravaged hers as he walked with her into his bedroom. As Marshall sat on the bed, Tamara's legs were still wrapped around his back. He moved his mouth from hers to her jawline, tickling her skin with tender nibbles and flicks of his tongue. His lips trailed to her ear, where he suckled on her earlobe. Tamara purred, the sensations overwhelming. Marshall's touch electrified her like no one's ever had.

His hands slipped beneath the bottom of her dress, sliding up her behind. Groaning, he looked at her. "What are you wearing?"

"Something I thought you would like."

"I do." He grinned as his fingers skimmed her bare behind. "I definitely do."

He eased onto his back, and Tamara went forward on his body as he did. His mouth found the area above her bosom, and he gently kissed the skin above her breasts. He attempted to access her body, but her clothes were in the way, so Tamara sat up and pulled the dress over her head and threw it onto the floor.

She looked down at Marshall, at his coy smile. His hands went to her bra, his fingers tracing the delicate edges of the fabric. Then he covered both breasts with his hands, the bra still between them, kneading the soft mounds. Tamara arched her back and moaned. She put her hands on his. She wanted to rip the bra out of the way. To have his mouth on her breasts immediately. There was a sense that she craved it.

Maybe even needed it.

"Please, play with my breasts." She wasn't sure who this wanton woman was who was speaking. She had never been this brazen. But there was something about Marshall's touch.

Not bothering to reach for the bra's clasp, she merely pushed it down and off of her breasts. Then she leaned forward again, positioning one breast over Marshall's face. He took it in his hand and guided her nipple into his eager mouth.

Tamara's sigh was long and rapturous. Oh, the pleasure!

He suckled her gently at first, but as her moans increased he picked up the pace. And when Tamara was panting from the delicious sensations, he took her other breast into his hand, pushed both mounds together and laved his tongue over both of her nipples at the same time.

"Oh, baby," she whimpered. "Oh, yes."

"I want to be inside of you." One of his hands trailed down her back, then smoothed over her bottom.

"Make love to me. Right now."

Tamara sat up, and Marshall fiddled with her thong, simply moving the fabric out of the way so that he could access her sweet spot. She looked at his face, intense with his desire. His eyes held hers as he entered her.

Tamara cried out, arching her back. Marshall's hands went to her nipples, and he played with them, making the sensations washing over her even more astounding. When she met his eyes again, he was still looking at her.

"Come here," he rasped and reached a hand up to her face. Slipping his fingers through her hair, he guided her face down to his. Then he kissed her, his tongue filling her mouth as his erection thrust into her.

Marshall kissed her until she could hardly breathe, his hips moving faster and faster. He responded to her sighs, repeating the same rotating thrust of his groin against her that she liked the most.

Tamara met his thrusts, and soon they were moving together at a frenetic pace. The two of them together were fire. And soon, that fire swallowed Tamara whole.

Her climax roared through her entire body. Knowing she had experienced her release, Marshall plunged into her steadily, his grunts coming shorter and faster. And when he came, he gripped her hips and threw his head back and let out a carnal growl.

He held her tight, their ragged breathing filling the air. Then he slipped both hands into her hair and held her face in place as he kissed her. It was a deep and lingering kiss.

And Tamara knew that she could get used to this.

Tamara and Marshall took some time out to eat, but mostly, they spent the day together naked. It was liberating. And it was fun—surely a Fourth of July weekend she would remember for years to come. Tamara never knew she could have so much fun just being naked in a house with a man. He chased her into the kitchen when she went to get wine, catching her and pinning her naked body against the wall, only to tease her with his lips and tongue. And though Tamara had felt a bit of trepidation, when dusk fell, she walked out onto the deck without a stitch of clothing on and went into the Jacuzzi with Marshall. As the sound of backyard fireworks went off, she and Marshall created their own fireworks in the warm, bubbly water.

Later, both of them wrapped in robes, Tamara lay on the sofa in his arms. He had just put in a DVD, and they were snuggling as the recent Denzel Washington thriller was set to begin.

"You know the other day when you mentioned that you'd like to get your own place sooner rather than later? A place where you and your son can have a bit of privacy? I think I have a solution for you."

Tamara angled her head to look at him. "Surely you're not suggesting that I move in with you." She might be enjoying her adult time with him, but moving in with Marshall would be a bad idea for Michael, especially this soon.

"No," Marshall said, and he chuckled softly. "That's not what I was going to say. My parents have bought a home in Arizona. It's on a golf course. A great location for them. Essentially, my father is retiring—though he still makes frequent visits to Cleveland. But the house they have here is sitting empty. Actually, it's the next court over." Marshall paused. "You and Michael could make use of it."

"A house in this neighborhood? How much is the rent?"

"You could house-sit for them. Someone there on a regular basis. I'd have to run it by them, but I think it could be a mutually beneficial arrangement."

Tamara shook her head. "You're offering me a place to live rent free? Why?"

"Because I like you. And because the house is sitting empty, and you're about to open a business. I'm sure my parents would love the idea of helping someone like you."

"Someone like me?"

"They've always given back to the community. They've supported many causes. And that includes helping people with ideas get their businesses started. That's what I mean."

Tamara laid her head back against his shoulder. "I don't know," she said. "I mean, let me think about it. I'm not necessarily ready to leave Callie and Nigel's place yet. But…I'll think about it."

"Okay. I mean, if you need it, it's there."

Tamara turned her attention to the movie, but her mind was whirring. Marshall was being sweet, and generous, but she didn't know how indebted to him she wanted to be. Yes, she was enjoying their time together, but she was all too aware that she didn't want to end up in too deep with him.

He was a nice distraction, a great way to reclaim a part of herself that had been lost. But more than that…? She wasn't ready to just jump into a relationship. She had her business and her son to consider.

"You know," Tamara began slowly, "what I said before… about a relationship…it still holds."

Marshall didn't respond. Then he reached for the remote control and paused the movie. "What are you saying?"

"I just…I just want to make sure that we both keep things in perspective. This is sex, and it's fun. But very soon I'm going to be absorbed in getting my business off the ground. And more important, my son settled in school. I guess I want to make sure that you're okay with that."

"So one minute I'm a player, the next I'm a guy who's going to propose marriage after having sex with a woman a couple of times?" Marshall raised an eyebrow, emphasizing his point that she had conflicting opinions of him.

"I'm just clearing the air, that's all. You're the one who's objected to the *player* label."

Marshall smoothed his hand over her hip. "You are the only woman I'm sleeping with."

The words made her heart flutter. But just as quickly as the sensation came over her, she tamped it down. She didn't want to be naive and even begin to hope where Marshall was concerned. Getting involved with him would veer her off the course she had set for herself.

"Gloria," Marshall muttered. "The woman I have to thank for your dismal view of me. How is she, by the way? Did I totally destroy her life with my player ways?"

"She's in Belgium."

"Really?"

"Yep. She left shortly after the two of you broke up. She married someone over there. She was offered a job there, took it and ultimately met her husband there. They have two kids, a boy and a girl."

"So I ran her out of the country? Is that what you're going to tell me?"

"Something you're used to?" Tamara asked playfully.

"Damn, your opinion of me."

"What can I say? You had a reputation."

Marshall repositioned himself on the sofa so that he was facing her. "Do tell."

"I don't think I need to be the one to tell you about your reputation," Tamara said. "You're the one who's lived this vastly scandalous life." She grinned to soften the blow of her words.

"Still, I want to hear from you."

"You're not serious, right?"

"Come on," Marshall told her. "I can take it. Tell me at least one juicy tidbit you heard about me."

"Well, since you want to know... One of the things I heard is that you had no less than one hundred lovers."

"One hundred!" Marshall roared with laughter. "Really?"

"That's what I heard."

"Wow. And that was years ago. Which would mean the number now would be even higher."

"At least five hundred," Tamara said. "Or what—is that number too low?"

He started to tickle her, until Tamara had to plead for mercy. "Okay, okay," she said, catching her breath when he subsided his assault. "So five hundred is wildly exaggerated, I take it?"

"Even one hundred is wildly exaggerated. I've had girl-friends, yeah. And some more casual flings. But nowhere near one hundred. How do people spew facts they can't possibly know?"

"I don't know. Just no more tickling," Tamara said, attempting to sound stern.

"Wow." Marshall shook his head. "I bet you think I've never had my heart broken."

"You don't strike me as the type who's had his heart broken."

"Interesting. Why not?"

"Because you always seem so easygoing. Happy-go-lucky. Like you've never experienced hurt."

"Goes to show how much you know," Marshall said, and his tone was soft. "I've been hurt, Tamara. More than once."

She stared into his eyes, surprised that she saw honesty there. She couldn't imagine Marshall being hurt but could easily see him in the role of the heartbreaker.

"Why do you look so surprised? You don't think I have feelings?"

"I...I guess...just everything I'd heard about you."

"Well, let me set you straight. Vivica was my high school girlfriend. I loved her. She was beautiful."

"Of course."

"And she was fun. We got along. She was my first love. I thought I was going to marry her. I stayed here for college, but she went to California. I bought her everything she could ever want or need. She liked the finer things, and I spoiled her. But hey, she was my girl. I was happy to do it. When she went to Berkeley, I often bought her airline tickets so she could come back and visit me. And I went down to see her as much as I could."

"Sounds nice."

"It was. Until the surprise visit I planned."

"Oh."

"Yeah, I went to see her. Didn't tell her I was coming. But when I showed up at her dorm room, I was the one who got the surprise. I found her in the room with another guy."

"Oh, no."

"Yep," Marshall said. He linked fingers with hers. "I was crushed. Devastated."

"What did you do?"

"Did I scream and holler and throw things around? Maybe punch the guy out?" Marshall shook his head. "Naw. It wasn't his fault. And as for Vivica, she wasn't worth it. Obviously, she'd been using me. I was heartbroken, yeah, but I realized that I had to move on. And it was better that I find out then that she was lying to me than later on."

"And the other person who broke your heart?"

Marshall's lips parted, but he didn't speak right away. When he did, he said, "Actually, she reminds me a lot of you."

Tamara's eyes widened in surprise. "Really? How so?"

"I suppose more in terms of your situations being similar. She'd been with an abuser. We met, and I really fell for her. I thought that I had loved Vivica, but Lisa…she was really it for me. I was a few years older. More mature. I knew what I wanted. Lisa was kind, giving. Really sweet. But I guess those qualities were what made her the type of person who wanted to nurture someone like the guy she'd been dating before we got together."

Tamara nodded, her stomach suddenly feeling queasy. She could relate. She had felt the need to nurture Patrick. To love him through his insecurities. To stick with him as he tried to become a better person. "I know what that's like," she said softly. "And no matter how much you love them, you can't free them of their demons." She paused. "What happened with Lisa?"

"I proposed. Then she started crying. At first I thought it was because she was happy. Until I realized she was far too upset. That's when she told me that she'd been talking to her ex. That she couldn't marry me. She was going back to him. I was devastated. I could almost handle her breaking up with me, just as long as she didn't go back to him. I knew he was bad news. But she…" Marshall released an emotion-filled sigh. "She thought she could save him."

He went silent, caught up in an unpleasant memory. Tamara stared at him, her heart rate picking up as she feared she knew how the story ended. "Marshall, what happened to her?"

"I admire your resolve, Tamara. You got out of your marriage. You testified against your ex. You got into therapy. That's invaluable. Lisa… She went back to her ex, and before I knew it, I heard the news story that he'd killed her."

Tamara gasped. "Oh, my God."

"Yeah," Marshall said softly. "That was tough. Really brutal."

For the first time, Tamara was seeing the not so happy-go-lucky side of Marshall. She could see the pain in his eyes even now, years after this had happened. And it made her realize that he wasn't the man she thought he was. At least, not the heartless person everyone had portrayed him to be.

He was a man of character and substance, and he was capable of deep emotions. She had wondered how he could be so happy all the time, but maybe that was the way he coped with his painful memories. It hadn't been right for her to judge him in a negative way.

"I'm sorry," Tamara told him. "It's obvious you cared about her very much."

Marshall merely nodded. Then he smoothed his fingers along Tamara's cheek, a tender movement. His eyes held hers, but he still said nothing, and Tamara could hardly breathe. Because in this moment, she was starting to truly become afraid of the feelings in her heart. Marshall was not the man she expected him to be, and that scared the heck out of her.

He planted his lips on her forehead, and then he said, "What about you? You think that I left a trail of broken hearts. But you just as easily could have."

"I didn't date a lot. I wasn't lying when I said I was an awkward teen. Guys didn't notice me. You included," she said and poked his belly. "Then I met Patrick…. I get that people don't understand why a woman stays. But there is a bit of them that's good, the way they love you…it's like you're the only person in the world. It's an intensity that maybe just isn't healthy. But you're caught up in it, and it feels like…like magic, in a way. So when they act out of jealousy, you tell yourself that somehow you're to blame. That you must have done something wrong," she stressed, remembering the arguments she'd had with Patrick when he'd believed that she had looked a certain way at a guy or that she'd been flirting. "You have seen the best of this person, so when they show you the worst, you remember how great they were. How much they loved you. And of course, with them blaming you for their irrational behavior, you know that as long as you change your ways, things can go back to the way you want them to be. Oh, they're very good at spinning the tale of just how much they love you."

Tamara closed her eyes pensively. A few beats passed before she could speak. Marshall continued to stroke her face. "I'm so glad that I can understand now why I got caught in that type of an abusive relationship. My biggest concern these days is Michael. I hope that what has happened with his father won't scar him forever."

"People say kids are resilient, and they really are. He seems like he's happy, adjusting well. I don't know him as well as you do, of course, but I'm guessing that he'll be just fine. In big part due to you."

That was when Tamara felt her eyes mist. She had come here for sex, but she was getting more than she'd bargained for.

Every moment she spent with him, Marshall was surprising her. And she wasn't sure she was prepared for that.

But for now, she would take it.

She looked into his eyes and offered him a little smile. "How about we watch that movie now?"

"Yeah."

Then she turned in his arms, and he draped his arm around her waist.

Tamara allowed herself to enjoy the here and now with a man who was turning out to be far more incredible than she had ever imagined.

Chapter 15

The next morning, Tamara awoke with a start. She bolted upright in the bed and looked at the clock on the night table.

10:09 a.m.

"Oh, my goodness. Michael..."

Beside her, Marshall made a groggy sound. Then he put an arm around her waist and said, "Huh, baby?"

"It's after ten. I wanted to get back to the house earlier than this, in case Callie and Nigel and the boys get home early today." She didn't want Michael to wonder where she had been.

Or worse, Callie.

"It's okay," Marshall said. "I doubt they'll be back until much later."

Tamara swung her feet off of the bed. "But just in case, I should leave."

Marshall moved closer to her, ensnaring her waist with both of his arms now. He pulled her back onto the bed and nuzzled his nose in her neck. "Oh, no, you don't. You don't get to leave until I've made you breakfast."

"I can eat at Callie and Nigel's house."

"So you're going to run out of my house again and refuse to sit down and have a meal with me in the morning? You're going to give me a complex."

Was she being obtuse? Would it be the end of the world if she came in after they arrived? They didn't have to know she'd spent the night with Marshall.

As she looked at Marshall's smiling face, she was swayed by his easy charm. "What are my choices? Cheerios or Frosted Flakes?"

"Oh, it's like that, is it?"

He began to tickle her, and Tamara's feet flailed and she writhed, trying to escape his torturous touch.

"Stop!" she begged.

"Take it back," Marshall told her.

"I'm sorry! I—I didn't mean it."

Finally, Marshall relented his fingers, and Tamara's laughter and heavy breathing began to subside. He kissed her softly on the lips. "You will definitely take it back once you get a chance to savor my culinary skills."

"All right, then. I'm prepared to be wowed."

And wowed she was, with fresh waffles topped with blueberries and whipped cream, and an omelet that was so fluffy it rivaled the best she had ever tasted. They ate on the back deck, overlooking the sprawling yard, and Tamara's gaze kept wandering to the hot tub, where they'd made love yesterday as though this backyard was a hedonistic paradise.

"Yeah," Marshall said, following her line of sight to the Jacuzzi. "That was fun. We can do it again if you want…"

"Not now," she told him. It was already after eleven, and she really wanted to get back to the house. "I really ought to be going."

Tamara left, hoping that when she got back to the house, it would be empty. But no such luck. The RV was in the driveway when she arrived.

She parked on the street and started into the house, her

stomach fluttering as she did. She knew that there would be questions.

No big deal, she told herself. There was no reason she couldn't have gotten up early and driven by the salon she was purchasing.

When she entered the house, Michael came charging toward her from the living room. "Mom!"

"Hey, sweetheart." She hugged him tightly. Even this short time away from him, she had missed him.

"I missed you," he said.

"I missed you, too." She leaned over to kiss the top of his head. "Did you have fun?"

"Uh-huh. I even caught a fish!"

"You did?"

"Yeah. But I felt bad, so we released it back into the water."

"That was nice of you."

Callie emerged from the hallway, followed by Kwame. "There you are."

"Yep. Here I am."

"Michael was worried about you. Wondered where you were. We tried your cell a few times, but it went straight to voice mail."

"Oh, that's strange. But I went out. Took a nice drive."

"For three hours?" Michael asked.

Tamara's stomach lurched. "You guys came back before nine?"

Callie nodded. "Michael missed you. Plus, we had an issue with the plumbing on the RV. We had to head out early."

"Oh. Sounds unpleasant." Tamara said nothing else, hoping there would be no further questions.

But the next thing she knew, there was a knock on the door. Then it opened, and Marshall entered.

Tamara's heart spasmed—especially when she noticed that he was carrying her cell phone in its pink glittery case. Even Michael would realize that the phone was hers.

"Marshall," Callie said. "What a pleasant surprise."

Tamara saw when Callie's eyes noticed the phone, and as she feared, Callie quickly looked at her. A knowing expression passed over her face.

"Marshall!" Michael ran over to him and hugged him.

Tamara swallowed.

"Hey, that's my mom's phone."

"Marshall offered to take me for breakfast this morning," Tamara said by way of explanation, walking toward him. "I can't believe I left my phone in the restaurant. Thanks for bringing it over."

"No problem." He passed her the phone, and as she took it, she quickly turned. Only to see Callie grinning at her devilishly.

"Marshall." Nigel, who had just come from the bedroom, smiled broadly when he saw his friend. "What's up?"

"Just dropped something off for Tamara," he said.

"Oh?" Nigel's eyebrows rose.

"We met for breakfast," Tamara explained. "I forgot my phone in the restaurant."

"Guess what?" Michael asked Marshall.

"What, buddy?"

"I caught a fish!"

"You did?"

"Yeah." Michael then relayed to Marshall the same story he had told Tamara. Once he was done, he asked, "You want to play soccer with me and Kwame in the backyard?"

"Michael, Marshall was kind enough to bring me my phone. But he probably has to go."

"I have nowhere to be," Marshall said, and Michael's face lit up. "Sure, we can go outside and play some soccer."

Michael bounded toward the patio door, followed by Kwame and Nigel. When Tamara and Callie were finally alone, Callie planted her hands on her hips and said, "Breakfast with Marshall, huh?"

Tamara swallowed, didn't quite meet Callie's eyes. "Yeah."

"Uh-huh." Callie's tone was ripe with skepticism. "Did you spend the night there?"

"Callie! Why would you ask me that?"

Callie pursed her lips. "Because I can see it all over your face." She stepped toward her, took her hands in hers and squeezed them. "Oh, my goodness!" she said in an excited whisper. "You and Marshall! You...*you were together!*"

"We..." Tamara couldn't form words. It was pointless trying to come up with a story to spin to Callie. She knew her too well.

"Does that make me a bad person?" Tamara asked, wrinkling her nose.

"Oh, my God!" Callie exclaimed. "You and Marshall!"

"Calm down," Tamara said, her gaze flying toward the patio door. "I don't want Michael to hear you."

"They're outside. They can't hear us. But just in case, let's go in your room." Callie led her by the hand down the hallway and into the bedroom she was using. Once there, she plopped down onto the bed and patted the spot beside her. "I want to hear *everything.*"

Tamara drew in a deep breath. "You were right. I was at his place last night."

"Oh, no no no. That's not anywhere close to the 'everything' I want to hear." Callie paused, her eyes widening. "How did this happen?"

Tamara swallowed, unsure what to say. How could she tell Callie that it had already happened...last week?

"Did he call you? Did you call him?" Callie prompted.

"He called me," Tamara said slowly. "He suggested we get together for dinner or something. Since I was here alone."

"I love it! Go on."

"And..." Tamara paused, inhaling deeply. "Obviously, we were both feeling some sort of attraction to each other. It started last week when we were spending so much time together."

"But what about the fact that you thought he was a player? After how you said he hurt your cousin, I never thought you would give him the time of day."

"It's not like I planned this," Tamara said, not sure what else to say. "It just… I don't know. He's a sexy guy. He's charming. And… Just being around him, my libido was alive again. So I thought…what the heck? It had been a *long* time, and there was a part of me that needed some…" She looked down, bashful. "You know."

"Girl!" Callie slapped her thigh. "And was it…as good as I imagine?"

"Oh, God, yes," Tamara blurted and then quickly covered her mouth, embarrassed to have answered so enthusiastically.

Callie laughed. "Good for you!"

"It was a good night," Tamara went on, feeling a flash of heat as she remembered their time in the Jacuzzi. "I saw a completely different side of Marshall."

"I'll bet!"

"No, I don't mean it like that. Though I saw that and then some," she added in a conspiratorial whisper.

Callie stamped her feet on the floor in rapid succession, her delight at this news obvious.

Tamara said, "I've labeled him as a player since the moment I saw him again, but I don't think he is. At least not anymore. He's really a caring, wonderful guy."

"Woo," Callie said, casting her a sidelong glance. "Are you saying—"

"Could it be anything more than that? No."

Callie frowned. "Oh, that's too bad."

"I have a goal, Callie. And that goal is to see my business off the ground. I don't have the time to devote to a relationship. Marshall… It was what I needed, and it was great. My opinion of him has certainly changed. I'm not against hooking up with him again." She smiled slyly.

"Good for you," Callie repeated. "You're actually beaming. Glowing. All that good stuff. After all you've been through, you certainly deserved a bit of fun."

"Of course, if Marshall hadn't come over when he did, I would've been able to keep my secret a little longer."

"Whether or not Marshall came by, I would have known that something happened with you. Like I said, you have this glow about you. I would've grilled you until you told me."

At one point, while sitting on the back deck and watching the kids, Michael ran up to Tamara. He was smiling from ear to ear.

"I think Marshall likes you," he announced.

Tamara's stomach tightened. "What?"

"I think Marshall likes you."

Tamara chuckled nervously. "Why would you say that?"

"Well, he took you on a date today."

"That was just because I was here alone. He figured it would be nice for us to go to breakfast together."

Michael was shaking his head, the smile still on his lips. "Mom, when a guy asks you out on a date, it's because he likes you."

He said that as though Tamara was utterly clueless, and she actually had to smile. "I'm sure he thinks I'm a nice person."

"You know what I think? I think he'd be a great dad."

Tamara's eyes bulged at her son's statement. For a moment, she wasn't sure what to say. Then she pulled him onto her lap and said, "I'm glad that you like Marshall and that you're enjoying spending time with him. But—"

"I want him to be my dad." Michael spoke with resolve.

Tamara truly had no clue what to say. She hadn't been in this situation before. After a moment, she said, "It's not that simple. It doesn't work that way."

He looked at her, disappointed. Tamara rubbed both of his arms. "You'll be seeing him a lot. So that's great. We're here in Cleveland now, so you can continue to have lots of fun with him."

Michael slid off of her lap, a small frown pulling at his lips. As a mother, a part of her wanted to tell him exactly what he wanted to hear. That sure, she and Marshall could get married and sail off into the sunset together and that they would become one happy family. But she did not want to mislead him or lie to him. The truth, no matter how hard to accept, was always the best option.

Michael ran back down onto the lawn. He went over to where Nigel and Marshall were working on the back shed. He offered to help, lifting the hammer and other tools as the men needed them.

It did make Tamara a little sad watching her son with Marshall and Nigel. It was so clear how much he craved a father-son relationship. And that wasn't wrong. She just wished that he'd been able to have it with his own father.

But life didn't always give you what you wanted, and Tamara knew that firsthand. Michael had to learn that lesson, as well.

It was just after two-thirty when Marshall announced that he had to head home so that he could quickly shower and get dressed for work. Tamara followed him outside so that she could speak to him alone.

He grinned at her, his ever-charming smile. "I really want to kiss you right now," he said.

"What were you thinking?" Tamara asked, ignoring his statement. "Thanks to you coming here minutes after I did with my phone, Callie figured things out. Now my son is talking about you liking me and that he wants you as a father." She stared at him hard, showing her displeasure. "This thing between us was supposed to be just that. Between us. The last thing I need is my son starting to have fantasies about you as his father."

"Because I'm such a bad guy, right?"

"That's not what I said. I'm trying to protect him. He's vulnerable. Obviously he's taking to you because you're showing him attention. I don't want him to be disappointed if things don't work out the way he wants them to."

"And you think he suddenly has these feelings because I brought you your phone?"

"He thinks you took me on a date!" Tamara said in a heated whisper.

"Michael is a smart kid. Did it ever occur to you he picked up on the vibe between us? Or that maybe he's just enjoying spending time with me, so it's naturally lending to his desire that you and I get together?"

"Whatever it is, you handled today's situation badly. You came traipsing in here with my phone, not at all thinking about how I would feel about you showing up the way you did."

"What I was thinking was that you probably wanted to have your phone and sooner rather than later. So when I realized that you had left it, I got in my car and started over here. It wasn't like I could call you," he added emphatically.

Tamara said nothing, just tightened her lips. He had a point, but she didn't want to concede it. She'd slept with him, yes, and now it seemed as though things were snowballing in a direction she wasn't prepared for.

"You know," Marshall began, "when people do someone a favor, it's customary to say 'thank you.'"

Then he turned and started toward his car. Tamara, suddenly fuming, charged after him. "I thought I made it clear that I didn't want a relationship. I thought you would realize that what's happening between us is supposed to be between *us*. Not my son, for goodness' sake. I can't have him thinking that you and I should be getting together. You ought to be apologizing to me, not giving me attitude."

Marshall stood at the door to his vehicle and faced her. "So far, all I've heard from you is what you want from me. You haven't asked what I want. And that's fine. I can take this at your pace. This can just be…whatever you want it to be. You have accused me of being a player and of being shallow. Yet I've been there for you. And I've been there for your son. Now you're upset because he's enjoying spending time with me? Either you want me to be a jerk or you don't. Make up your mind."

Tamara swallowed. "Tomorrow, I will get to the dealership

In the end, she had been stuck in that unhappy place with her abuser. Marshall knew that Tamara was not stuck in the same way Lisa had been, but maybe her experience with her ex would forever prevent her from truly trusting a man again.

Hadn't he told himself to begin with that this was the danger of dating someone like Tamara? And yet, he had been so fiercely drawn to her. When they had made love, the experience had been beyond amazing. How could he not have wanted more?

A slow jam began to play on the radio, and Marshall quickly changed the station, not in the mood to hear anything with a romantic sentiment. He hadn't gotten involved with Tamara thinking that he wanted more, but considering the intensity of their attraction and how easily they had connected once she let her guard down, he had been open to the possibilities between them. But maybe what he needed to do was be just like her and have a completely nonchalant attitude toward sex.

He remembered the look in her eyes, how upset she had been at the idea that her son looked up to him as a father figure. That hurt. Because it told him that the niggling of hope in his heart that maybe Tamara might be someone who could be in his life for a long time was simply a wish built on sand.

And now the tide had come in and washed the sand away.

Reality settled over him. She wanted to slow things down. She wanted her space.

What could Marshall do but give it to her?

Over the next few weeks, Tamara busied herself with her work. She had a ton to do in order to get her shop set up, which she was planning to open in early August. There were state tests she had to take to prove she had the sufficient knowledge and expertise to be a stylist. There had been a lot of running around and scrambling in order to meet her goal of an early August opening date. Sure, she thought of Marshall from time to time, but she was able to keep him on the back burner of her thoughts because she was staying extremely busy.

Marshall had come by the house a few times, and Michael had always been elated. But he had kept his distance from her.

She would be lying to herself if she said it hadn't hurt on some level, but she had always known that she didn't want Marshall to be a distraction where her plans were concerned. Yes, there were some nights when she had been so hot and bothered that if she didn't have a smidgen of pride, she would have called and asked if she could come over. But she had refrained.

What had bothered Tamara was that, a few days ago, Michael had asked her why she didn't like Marshall anymore. When she told him he was wrong, he cited the proof that when he came around, they didn't really speak to each other.

Which only made her think about the fact that Marshall had said Michael had likely picked up on the vibe between them, and that was what had led him to express his feelings about wishing Marshall could be his father.

Tamara had jumped to the conclusion that Michael learning of her date with Marshall had set those thoughts in motion, but perhaps Marshall had been right. Though her son was only eight, he was very perceptive.

Tamara looked around her salon, wondering why her thoughts had ventured to Marshall. Sighing softly, she tried to push him from her mind and concentrate on her progress. All of the equipment she had ordered was in place. The shop looked elegant, with its decorative mirrors and brand-new light fixtures. It looked exactly like the kind of place where she would like to come and get her hair done. She had painted the walls a shell-pink color and adorned them with framed photos by local artists and framed inspirational poems.

When Tamara heard a knock at her store door, she jerked her head toward the glass. She was stunned to see Marshall standing outside. He was with another male.

Tamara put down the paintbrush, which she had been using to touch up the baseboards, and walked toward the door. She unlocked it and then pulled it open. "Marshall?"

"Tamara."

"What are you doing here?" Tamara asked. Her eyes flitted between Marshall and the man standing beside him. Callie and/or Nigel must have given him the location to the salon.

"This is James," Marshall explained. "He's a cousin of mine."

Callie narrowed her eyes, not understanding. "I'm not open for business yet," she told him. "And even if I were, I don't have a barber."

"That's what I heard," Marshall said, "and that's why we're here." When Tamara's eyes narrowed further, he went on. "James is a barber. He's very skilled. His last arrangement recently ended, and he's looking for a place to work."

Tamara folded her arms. "And you thought I would want to hire him?" Couldn't he have called her first? Run this by her?

"I know you planned for this to be a female hair salon, but if James can rent a chair from you, that would bring in more business. I think having a male clientele would serve you well. Help your business grow. James, why don't you tell Tamara about your experience. I don't need to be the one doing all of the talking."

Tamara's jaw stiffened. Marshall thought she needed his help to make her business grow? She was going to do this on her own. She didn't need Marshall telling her how to do her business, how to garner more sales. She had her own ideas, and her vision was for this to be a salon for women only. Even the color she had put on the walls catered to that vision.

James extended his hand. Tamara took it, and he shook it. "Nice to meet you, Tamara. I've been in Cleveland for fifteen years doing hair. Like Marshall said, I can rent a chair from you, maybe set up in the back or in the front—wherever would work best for you—and bring in some more business. It would be a win-win, as I'm looking for a new place to work out of. And for you it would mean more money." When Tamara said nothing, he grinned and added, "I'm very talented."

"I don't doubt that," Tamara said. Her jaw was still tense.

She glanced at Marshall, saw that he wasn't looking directly at her.

Of course he wasn't.

Tamara sucked in a deep breath, trying to hide her annoyance. "Thank you for the suggestion. But right now I'm not ready to figure that aspect out. I'll have to see how it goes once I get started. I'm meeting with a couple of female stylists, because I anticipate needing some help. I really didn't give any thought to a male clientele, and truthfully I'm not sure if that's something I want to do. But thank you. I'll take your card and your information, and if I change my mind, I will definitely let you know."

James looked a bit disappointed, but he nodded his understanding. "Fair enough."

She bent to pick up her paintbrush again, all but dismissing them. "Now, if you will excuse me, I have work to do."

Marshall and James left the store, and only once they were out did Tamara realize Marshall had not said goodbye. Nor had she, of course.

She was perturbed with his presumptuousness. He should have called her before just coming in here expecting her to offer his cousin a job.

About fifteen minutes later, Tamara was at the back of the shop on her knees painting a section of the baseboards when she heard the door chimes sing again. Her heart began to flutter.

Marshall...

But when she looked over her shoulder, it wasn't Marshall entering the shop. It was a young man, tall and lanky, and goose bumps quickly popped out on her skin.

Tamara got to her feet. "Can I help you?" she asked as coolly as she could.

The man was walking toward her at a quick pace, and Tamara's back stiffened. "Yeah, you can," he said, his voice low. "You can give me all your money."

The next part happened fast. He lunged at her, caught her

in a headlock. Tamara screamed. The only thing she had in her hand was the paintbrush, and she attempted to hit her attacker with it over the head.

"Where's your money?" he demanded.

"I...I don't have any here. I haven't opened yet."

"Where is it?" He tightened his grip.

Tamara clawed at his hands, terrified. Then her survival instinct kicked in. She remembered exactly what she had learned in the self-defense classes she had taken after Patrick had been locked up. She steeled her elbow and jerked it backward, hitting the man in his solar plexus as hard as she could. He hadn't been prepared for it, and her blow had knocked him off of his axis. His hand loosened, and she quickly squirmed free and faced him, wasting no time in punching his nose upward with an open palm.

Then she stood in front of him, her arms in a protective yet offensive stance, ready for whatever action he might take. She only hoped he didn't have a weapon of any kind, because she wasn't prepared for that.

He looked at her, his eyes registering surprise and almost a little bit of delight. "Oh, so you're a tough one."

Tamara went into full attack mode. She kicked him in his chest and knocked him backward. There was no time to mess around. She had to take offensive action in order to get the upper hand.

He wasn't prepared for her assault, and he fell backward onto his butt. Tamara was certain she'd heard his head hit the floor. Then she ran for the phone at the front and punched in 911.

"911 operator. What's your emergency?"

"There's an intruder in my store!" Tamara yelled into the phone. "He just attacked me! Please help me!"

But the man was already bolting through the door. He took off down the street.

When Tamara hung up the phone, she ran to the door and bolted it shut. Then, with her chest heaving and her head pounding, she slid down the length of the door and crumpled into a heap on the floor.

And then she burst into tears.

Marshall got the call from Nigel about the attack on Tamara shortly after he returned home.

"What do you mean someone attacked her at the salon?" Marshall asked, all the air leaving his lungs in a rush. "When?"

"It happened around one o'clock. She said someone walked into the salon demanding money."

"What?" His heart froze in his chest. "I was there shortly before one." The attack must have happened minutes after he and James had left. Damn, if only they had stayed. If only Marshall had done what his mind had told him to do and gone back in to speak to Tamara. He'd missed her over the past weeks, but the look she'd had on her face when he and James had shown up had told him that she hadn't missed him. Her reception had been cold, and Marshall had figured that she wouldn't appreciate him going back into the salon to talk to her. "I was there, damn it. I was there and I left."

"The good news is, she's okay," Nigel said. "She fought back. Apparently gave the attacker more than he expected. She's more shaken up than anything."

"Is she at the hospital?"

"No. She refused medical treatment. She gave her statement to the police, and I just brought her home."

"I'm on my way."

Why hadn't she called him? That was the thought that plagued Marshall as he rushed to Nigel's place. He had stopped by to see her, and the attack had happened not too long after he and James had left. She had to have realized that he wasn't too far away. She could have called 911, then called him immediately after so that he could rush to her side.

Marshall had his car door open even before he fully had his car in Park. He bounded out of the car and ran to the front door. Turning the knob, he found it open and rushed into the house.

His eyes went to the right, past the foyer into the living room, where he saw Tamara curled up on the sofa, looking wary. Michael sat beside her, his arms curled around her waist. Callie sat on her other side.

Marshall hurried over to her. Callie got up, and he sat in the spot she'd vacated. "Are you okay?"

She nodded weakly.

It hurt him to see her in pain, more than he would have expected. "This happened minutes after James and I left?"

"Yeah. In fact, I thought it was you coming back. I hadn't locked the door, and the next thing I know, this guy was coming in. He demanded money. At first I froze, but when he grabbed me in a headlock, the self-defense I'd learned in Florida kicked in. I was able to fight him off. I think I hurt him, actually. He ran out of the store when I was calling for the police."

"Thank God." Marshall wrapped his arms around her and cradled her face, relieved to see for himself that she was unhurt. He couldn't bear to think of the very real possibility that this situation could've had a very different outcome.

His eyes ventured to Michael, who looked terrified. For him, this incident must have brought back painful memories of the abuse they had suffered at the hands of his father. "Hey, bud," Marshall said softly. "How are you doing?"

"I'm scared."

"Your mom's tough. Remember that, okay? She's tough, and she's gonna be just fine."

Michael nodded. "She said that she punched the bad guy in the face."

"I'll bet she gave it to him good, too." Marshall smiled. "Can I talk to your mom alone for a minute?"

"Okay." Michael seemed a lot more at ease now. He stood and went to Callie, who'd extended her hand to him.

Marshall waited until they were outside on the deck, where they joined Nigel and Kwame. Then he turned back to Tamara. His face grew serious, and he ground out a frustrated breath.

"Why didn't you call me?" he asked. "I'd just been there. I wasn't far. And heck, I'm a cop."

Tamara exhaled loudly. "I—I didn't think. I called 911, and then I lost it."

Marshall gritted his teeth. "Are you sure that's the only reason? Come on, Tamara. You must know that I care about you. That if you were in trouble, I would help you."

"I just didn't think. I was scared. It wasn't personal."

A few moments passed. Then Marshall asked, "Are you sure you're okay?"

"I'll be fine. I just hope that jerk doesn't come back."

"You got a good look at him, right? Were you able to give a description to the police?"

"I did. But they'd like me to go to the station in order to look through photos. I told them I'd do that tomorrow. Today... I'm just drained."

"That makes sense. If you want, I can go with you."

"I'll let you know."

"I'm kicking myself for not staying there longer with you," Marshall said. "Or wishing I'd come by just a bit later. It wouldn't have happened if I had been there."

"You never know when these things are going to happen. Or who knows if the guy was watching the salon? He should have known that I wasn't open for business if he was watching me, though." Tamara sighed. "I don't know. I guess anything can happen at any time. I'm just glad the self-defense I learned helped me to fight him off."

"Do me a favor—pick up some pepper spray. A little can of it. So that if it happens again, you can spray the perpetrator. Add that to your self-defense arsenal."

"I will."

Marshall looked down at her and wanted more than anything to kiss her. But a quick glance toward the patio door told him that wasn't advisable. Because Michael stood at the door, peering in, a small grin playing on his lips.

Chapter 17

Ten days had passed, and the man who had attacked Tamara had not been caught. She hadn't recognized him in an array of photos of known suspects, and while that unnerved her, she went ahead with her plans to open the salon. The way she saw it, he'd come to rob her, hadn't succeeded, and she doubted that he would be back.

As promised, Callie's sister Natalie had helped plan a big event to celebrate the opening of Tamara's salon, which she had decided to name Illuminessence. The event was scheduled for that night, the Thursday before the opening. There had been a write-up in the paper, announcements on the local news stations—all thanks to Natalie's skills and connections as an event planner, not to mention the fact that with Deanna performing, the event had generated huge buzz.

Tamara was thrilled. Excited and anxious. She had found two experienced stylists who would work with her. She was looking forward to doing the hair of the women in Cleveland. It was a far cry from real estate, but Tamara had never felt more thrilled about a career choice in her life.

The salon doors were due to open at six, with hors d'oeuvres and champagne being served for the VIP guests, who were scheduled to tour the establishment first. After that, it was open to the public on a first come, first serve basis. The crowd outside of the salon had started assembling before five.

"You look amazing," Callie told her. She, her sisters, the stylists she had hired, as well as the waitstaff for the event were all in the building and ready for the first guests to arrive.

"Thank you." Tamara glanced to the right, at her reflection. She had styled her hair in an updo, with a few drop curls framing one side of her face. Natalie had taken her shopping to pick up a dress provided by a local designer her husband knew—and free of charge. Free samples and coupons had been provided for the gift bags by other local business owners, all of which made Tamara feel incredibly welcome to the community.

The dress, a shimmery black number that hugged her curves, made her look incredible. A professional makeup artist had created a dramatic look to match her attire, including a string of pearls borrowed from a nearby jeweler, as well as a stunning multicolored sparkling bracelet.

The time ticked down. Five minutes before six, Tamara went to open the door.

Before long, the first guests arrived, the city's mayor accompanied by his wife. Other important guests soon followed. Deanna sang a variety of songs as the champagne flowed and the food trays made the rounds. Tamara introduced herself to everyone and made pleasant conversation, with Natalie by her side much of the time to let her know who was who.

"Great," Natalie said, when she saw the news crews arrive. "Right on time. All the important people are here, and so are the cameras. Come Saturday, the city of Cleveland are going to be rushing this salon, girl!"

"From your lips to God's ears," Tamara said with a smile.

An hour and a half later, there was a buzz of happy chatter in the room. The event was in full swing, and Tamara was elated to be conversing with countless numbers of the city's women. Sure, some had likely come here simply out of curiosity, happy with their stylists and not at all interested to make a change. But for those who didn't have stylists, she hoped they would be willing to give her salon a try.

Tamara couldn't help but grin as she gazed around the crowded room. Her dream was coming alive before her very yes. She would eternally be grateful to Callie and her sisters or helping to drum up all of this support and media attention. She could have never pulled off an event like this on her own.

The door chimes sang, and Tamara looked in the direction of the front door to see her son rushing toward her. "Mom!"

He threw his arms around her waist, and she had to grip his shoulders in order not to trip.

"Hey, baby," Tamara greeted him.

"You look beautiful!"

"Thank you." Tamara stroked Michael's cheek. "Nigel brought you here?" She looked past the crowd to see outside the front window, and when she saw Marshall standing outside, her heart began to race.

"Marshall and Nigel brought me," Michael explained. "Kwame's outside, too."

Tamara's eyes met Marshall's. Immediately she felt an undeniable jolt of desire. Good Lord, he looked amazing. Dressed in black jeans, a blazer, and shirt that was unbuttoned at the collar, he looked nothing short of a male model.

Maybe it was the sexual charge at seeing Marshall looking so handsome, but she was glad that he was here. Glad because they hadn't really spoken much since the attack. She had been busier than ever with getting her salon under way, so while they had exchanged a few texts and spoken briefly the times he stopped by the house, they certainly hadn't talked about anything of consequence.

Now, seeing him again, she felt the same intense attraction to him she had before any of the conflict between them had emerged.

"Come say hi," Michael said.

"Why isn't he coming in?" Tamara asked.

But she soon got her answer. Because when she got to the front door, she saw that sitting at Marshall's feet was a large golden retriever. Kwame was beside the dog, petting it happily.

"Hello," she greeted Nigel, Kwame and Marshall briefly. Her elation over seeing her son and Marshall temporarily forgotten, her eyes narrowed on the dog. "What is that?"

"It's a dog, Mom."

"I—I know that. What I mean is, why is it here? Why is it at my event?"

"This is Sherlock," Marshall explained. "My friend and his wife have gone off for a couple of days, so I'm watching Sherlock until they get back."

"That dog cannot come in my salon."

"I wasn't planning to bring him in."

"Good." Tamara swallowed. Suddenly the dog moved forward, and she instantly jerked backward. She stumbled on her heel, and Marshall quickly reached for her, catching her by her upper arm and preventing her from falling.

"I hate when dogs jump at me," she said, her breathing growing ragged.

"Sherlock's well behaved," Marshall said. "He just wanted to nuzzle his nose against your hand to greet you."

Tamara forced a deep breath into her lungs. "Nigel, are you coming inside?"

"Naw. The boys wanted to see how the event was going, so we decided to pop by. You look incredible, by the way."

Tamara smiled. "Thank you."

"Yes," came Marshall's deep voice, and she turned to him. His eyes roamed over her slowly, and she could see the craving in their depths. "You look…you look stunning."

Tamara's cheeks flamed. Hearing Marshall's compliment made her feel like the most beautiful woman in the world. "Thank you."

The dog began to move again, and Tamara flinched. "Are you really that afraid of dogs?" Marshall asked.

"I used to deliver newspapers. 'Nuff said."

Marshall handed the dog's leash over to Nigel. "Why don't you take Sherlock and the boys back to the car. I'll be there in a few."

"'Bye, Mom," Michael said.

Tamara said her goodbyes to her son, Kwame and Nigel. Then she turned to face Marshall.

"You really do look amazing," he said. "Your makeup. Your dress. You're ravishing."

Tamara gave him a bashful smile. "Thank you."

Suddenly, Marshall took her by the hand and led her around to the side of the building, out of the view of Nigel and the boys and anyone in the salon. Then he slipped an arm around her waist and pulled her close.

"Damn, I've missed you."

"I…I've missed you, too."

"Have you?" Marshall asked. He trailed his nose along her cheek. "Or have you been too busy to think about me?"

"I haven't stopped thinking about you," she said softly. Tamara could feel his warm, steady breaths on her cheek. Even that turned her on.

"Yes," he said. "I can feel it—your desire for me." His voice was low and raspy. "I didn't know if you'd found a way to get over it. But I still feel it." He trailed his fingers up her arms. "This desire is like a tangible thing. It has a life of its own."

Tamara could only draw in slow, even breaths in an attempt to calm her racing heart. He was right, absolutely. Every time she was around him, her longing for him took over.

His fingers trilled her skin as they moved up farther, finally reaching her jawline. When they got to the point of her chin, he angled her face upward. "I have missed you." He rubbed his groin against her. "Like, really, really missed you."

A shaky sigh escaped Tamara's lips as heat filled her body. "My…my event…"

"Are you really thinking about that right now?"

Hell, no. She was thinking how she wanted to run off with Marshall and get naked.

"Are you?" he asked.

"No."

"What are you thinking about?" he asked and brushed his lips against her cheek.

Her chest was heaving. "I'm thinking that I want...that I want to be alone with you."

"I want to touch you. I want to kiss you. But if I kiss you, everyone will know when you go back inside."

Tamara stared up at him, desperate to have his lips on hers, yet knowing one of his kisses would most definitely ruin her makeup.

Instead of kissing her, he brought a hand to her breast and squeezed. As he did, they both moaned.

"Okay, I can't do this. Not here."

And then he planted a soft, lingering kiss on her forehead. It was a promise of what would come later.

"I can't even see you tonight," Tamara said, a little whine to her voice. "With everyone here, and all I have to do... The next two days are going to be very busy and exhausting before I officially open my doors for business. But, on Sunday, I have to be in Toronto. I don't know. Maybe you could come with me...?"

"Toronto?" Marshall asked.

"I'm going there to take a course on the process of the new type of fusion extensions. It starts Sunday, continues Monday. But you normally have to work on Monday—"

"I'll take a vacation day."

Tamara's lips curled in a smile. "You will?"

"A couple days alone with you? In a hotel?

Now she beamed from ear to ear. "I plan to leave Saturday evening."

"The course starts on Sunday?"

"Yes."

"Then maybe we can stop in Niagara Falls Saturday night. Get one of those rooms with a heart-shaped Jacuzzi tub…"

The mention of Jacuzzi had Tamara's most feminine place thrumming. "We could maybe swing that."

Marshall then kissed the side of her mouth, making sure to avoid her lipstick. "Yeah. We most definitely can."

Good Lord, Tamara thought her body would explode. She couldn't take any more of being around him without being able to kiss and touch him in the explicit manner she craved.

He eased back, grinning down at her, as if pleased that he had her all but coming undone.

"We'll be in touch, then?"

"Yes. For sure."

Marshall took her hand and then walked her back around to the front of the salon. Glancing down the street, Tamara saw Nigel standing beside his vehicle. Kwame and Michael were taking turns tossing a stick to the dog. Tamara didn't bother to pull her hand free from Marshall's, not even when Michael looked over his shoulder at her. He'd disappeared with her around the side of the building—what was the point in pretending that there wasn't something going on between her and Marshall?

And now they were going on a weekend trip together. Tamara was excited about the idea of immersing Marshall into her life in a more meaningful way. Maybe it was the success of tonight and the fact that her hopes and dreams were coming together. But she was open to the possibility of furthering her relationship with Marshall. She was at a point where she knew she was going to want more if they continued having a physical relationship. Some people could sleep with partners with no strings attached, no problem. Tamara wasn't one of those people.

"See you later, beautiful," Marshall said.

Tamara grinned at him. "See you."

Then she went back into the salon and enjoyed the remain-

der of the party, thrilled at how everything was coming together for her.

It was hours later, when everyone was gone and she was
closing up, that she found a note on the desk at the reception
area.

No one wants you here.
Take your spotlight and go back where you came from.
You've been warned!

Chapter 18

On Saturday afternoon, Tamara and Marshall set off for Niagara Falls. Marshall did the driving, which Tamara didn't mind. It allowed her to sit back, put her feet up and relax.

The conversation between them was easy, and the flirting was fun. Marshall held her hand often and even leaned across the seat to sneak in a kiss at one point. Tamara felt as though they were developing a real relationship. She'd told Marshall more than once that she didn't have time for a relationship, and she wondered if—at least to him—what they were doing was still in the *fun* category. For her, things had definitely changed, and she wasn't quite sure when.

Maybe it had been when he'd come rushing to the house after the attack, and the obvious concern he'd had for her. He had seemed out of sorts and crushed that he hadn't been at the store at the time. He hadn't yet told her if he had feelings for her or not—but with her constantly reminding him that she wasn't interested in a relationship, she couldn't really blame him.

As Tamara's gaze wandered out the window, her mind drifted back to the day of the attack and the fact that the perpetrator was still at large. She then wondered if there was any possibility that the note she'd received at her salon could be connected to that attack.

She hadn't told Marshall about it, and a part of her wondered if she should. She had been on such a high after the launch party, only to receive that ominous note. It had worried her that someone who had been inside had obviously been the one to leave it for her. But she had allayed her concerns with the idea that it had probably been left by a competitor who was threatened by a new salon opening up nearby.

"So, are you going to tell me where we're staying?" Tamara asked Marshall, trying to push the ugly note from her mind. He'd told her that he wanted to make the arrangements for a hotel in Niagara Falls, and he'd seemed so excited at the prospect that she had let him.

"All I'm going to say is that you'll love it. You know Niagara Falls is the honeymoon capital of the world. So there are some pretty amazing suites for couples that are newly wed."

"Newlyweds…" Tamara's voice trailed off, and her stomach tickled.

"Well, they don't stipulate that you have to be married." He squeezed her hand, which he was already holding. "Good thing for us."

Late evening when they arrived in Niagara Falls, as promised, the room was outstanding. Marshall hadn't opted for a big-name hotel. Rather, he'd booked them at a boutique hotel, which, from the moment they entered, oozed luxury.

Their room was extremely large, with a kitchen and a separate living room—in addition to the bedroom with a large, heart-shaped bed. Rose petals adorned the bedcover, and on the night table was a carafe on a tray, with a bottle of chilling champagne and two champagne flutes.

"Wow, this is gorgeous!" Tamara exclaimed.

Marshall wandered over to the bed and bounced down onto

it, testing its comfort level. Tamara headed around a corner and into the bathroom—where she stopped in her tracks.

The fixtures were luxurious, the marble sleek. But the heart-shaped Jacuzzi tub was undoubtedly the star of the room.

"Marshall!" Tamara called.

Suddenly, she felt his arms encircling her waist from behind. "I'm right here, baby."

"Look at this tub! You could easily fit four people in there!"

"Lots of room to play," Marshall said. His voice had grown husky, and Tamara wasn't surprised when he turned her in his arms and brought his mouth down on hers.

Tamara's body exploded with heat. It seemed like forever since she'd been waiting to feel his touch again. She parted her lips on a sigh, eager to taste his tongue. But instead of deepening the kiss, Marshall's lips moved from her mouth to the underside of her jaw, near her ear. He kissed her there, softly. Then his lips moved an inch forward, and he kissed her there. He continued that pattern until he was at the tip of her chin, and from there he flicked out his tongue and trailed it down to the hollow of her neck.

Tamara gripped his shoulders and arched her back. There was no doubt about it—the man knew how to kiss. He knew that kissing wasn't relegated to the mouth alone. And he definitely knew that his lips on her skin, especially on her neck, set her body on fire.

She thought his mouth might venture lower, to her bosom, but instead his mouth sought hers again. There was no need to rush. They had hours to indulge in carnal pleasure.

Marshall drew her bottom lip between his and suckled her mouth until she felt weak in the knees.

Pulling back his head, he glanced down at her. A grin formed on his mouth. "What do you think of this room?" he asked.

"It's beautiful. Romantic." She stroked his face. "It's perfect."

"Which part would you like to take advantage of first?" Marshall asked in a lower tone.

"Filling the tub will take too long," she said, her voice raspy, "because I want to do you now."

"You can't wait, huh?"

Tamara shook her head. "Not a moment longer."

Marshall scooped her into his arms, and she giggled as he swept her across the room to the bed. And as he lowered her onto it, she looked up at him expectantly. Her chortling subsided as their eyes held. It was a lingering look, filled not just with longing, but something else—perhaps tenderness?

Tamara released a shaky breath. Suddenly, the significance of being in a honeymoon suite surrounded by everything meant for lovers truly hit her. This was the moment where, if her past had any hold over her, she would feel anxiety that could not be quelled. Instead, what she felt as she looked up at Marshall was that maybe fate had given her a second chance at love.

He came onto the bed beside her, leaning on his side while she lay on her back. His hands went to the top of her shirt, where he first teased her skin with his fingers before reaching for the first button. Slowly and delicately, he undid the buttons one by one. Tamara wanted him to rip his shirt off, get her naked as quickly as possible, but he was taking his time, drawing out the pleasure by the simple act of undressing her.

With her blouse undone, he pushed the fabric over her shoulders. She eased up so that he could nudge it off of her shoulders completely. Then his hands went back to the area above her breasts, gingerly skimming the full mounds of her flesh.

"I swear, I can't get enough of looking at you," he said.

"And I can't get enough of you touching me."

Marshall leaned forward, bringing his mouth to her body to explore the areas his fingers just had. His lips tantalized her skin as they gently kissed the area between her breasts, then each mound and then her abdomen.

Tamara's stomach fluttered as desire filled her body. She

smoothed her palm over his closely cropped hair. She drank in the very masculine sight of his muscular biceps, loving how they flexed as his arms were propped up on the bed.

His eyes met hers. There was no charming smile, just a look of intensity. He kissed her belly one more time before starting to undo the front of her jeans. He wrestled with the button, but freed it after a few seconds. Then he unzipped the jeans and shimmied them over her hips.

Tamara eased up and reached for the hem of her panties, but Marshall said, "No. Let me do it. I want to take off all of your clothes."

So she stayed still and let out a little gasp when he gently flipped her over onto her stomach. Then he pulled the panties over her behind—stopping to kiss her bottom—and then down her legs. Once it was off, Tamara heard his carnal moan.

Angling her head, she looked over her shoulder at him. This time, she was the one to flash a little smile. It was a smile that said she felt a charge of sexual power.

Soon, his hands were on her back, unfastening the clasp of her bra. Tamara eased up, and he pushed the fabric off of her shoulders. Then, spinning her over, he took the bra off completely and tossed it aside.

Now Tamara was naked on the bed, and Marshall stood tall so that he could look down at her, his eyes drinking in every part of her body, heating her skin as effectively as his touch. His yearning for her was etched on his face.

"Look at how beautiful you are. You're like a piece of priceless art. To be admired. I swear, I could never grow tired of looking at you."

Tamara's body quivered at his words. Her nipples tightened without him even touching her. His look alone was like a heated caress. Just observing the way he was studying her had her aroused beyond measure.

"The only problem is, I know I can't just look without touching."

"Good. Because I want you to touch."

Marshall's eyes widened as Tamara stood. Planting a hand
on his chest, she urged him onto the bed. He sat, his eyes holding hers. Taking a step forward, Tamara planted a knee on the
bed on the outer area of his right thigh. Then she planted her
other knee around his opposite thigh. As she straddled him,
she brought her mouth down onto his. She took his face in her
hands and held it tightly as she kissed him. It was a gentle, soft
teasing kiss, but one full of heat and passion. One that spoke
volumes of her desire for him.

"Baby." A growl emanated in his chest.

Tamara guided him onto his back and spread her naked body
over his fully clothed one. She pressed her breasts against his
chest, enjoying the feel of his cotton shirt against her skin. And
loving the power that came from knowing that at this moment
she had complete control over him.

She hadn't felt this kind of feminine control in her life before Marshall. She felt like a temptress, a seductress. The most
beautiful woman on the planet. The way Marshall looked at
her, and the sounds that escaped him, made her feel incredibly desirable.

She ravaged his mouth now, and his hands gripped her waist
as his fingers splayed over her behind. He then thrust his hips
upward, gyrating against her, and she could feel the evidence
of his desire rock hard against her womanhood.

He began to kiss her back with equal ferocity, and suddenly, he was spinning her over so that she was on her back.
His mouth moved from her lips down her neck almost with
desperation, seeking and then finding one of her nipples. He
drew the taut peak into his mouth and suckled. Tamara gasped
at the explosive feelings.

"I love the way you respond to me," Marshall said. "We're
so good together."

Tamara mewled softly and arched her back. And when Marshall's mouth moved to her other breast, she knew she'd found
a piece of heaven.

* * *

Marshall would never tire of the wanton response Tamara gave him every time he touched her. Lord, she was beautiful. And not just on the outside but on the inside. Being here with her like this, he knew that he couldn't imagine her not being in his life.

No doubt, he had enjoyed making love to her, but there was more to it than their physical connection. Even in the weeks she had pulled away from him, he hadn't been himself—and it hadn't been simply because he wanted her in his bed. But now she was back in his arms, a place that Marshall knew he wanted her to be for the long term.

Glancing upward, he saw an expression of pure erotic bliss on her face. She had a finger in her mouth, and her eyes were tightly closed.

His groin tightened. Then he encircled one of her nipples with the tip of his finger. "You like when I do this?"

"I love it."

"You know I could stay here with you like this all day and all night. Nothing would give me more pleasure than to give you pleasure for hours and hours and hours."

Tamara moaned. "Really?"

"You must know that." He stroked her nipple and then blew on it gently before taking it in his mouth again. He drew it in deep, as though trying to swallow it, and when he saw Tamara grip the sheets, that was all the reward he needed. He wanted to give her everything. He wanted to satisfy her until her body was completely spent and she couldn't take any more of it.

He wanted to please her so that thoughts of any other man were permanently erased from her mind.

"I can't take any more of this teasing, Marshall. Make love to me."

"I will. I will, baby."

Marshall loved the feel of her nipples in his mouth. But more so, he loved how she reacted to him. He'd meant it when he said he could stay in bed with her day and night and not get tired.

In fact, one day and one night wasn't enough time for him to be with Tamara.

He kissed the undersides of her breasts and then went down her rib cage, trailing his fingers along her skin as he did. He felt her body quiver beneath his touch. When he reached her belly button, he dipped his tongue into it and then softly sucked it.

Tamara's hands were on his shoulders now, her fingers digging into his skin.

Marshall's mouth went lower still, to that sweet spot. The most feminine part of her. There, he took his time pleasuring her until her back was arched, her legs clenched around his face, and she was crying out his name.

He didn't relent until every bit of her orgasm escaped from her body. Only then did he stand, his eyes never leaving that beautiful body of hers, which was left trembling from his touch. Marshall made quick work of taking off his clothes. He got a condom from his pocket to use as he had when he'd made love to her before. But for the first time, he felt the longing to make love to her without any barrier between them. It was an impulse that he was unfamiliar with.

Seeing Tamara lying there, writhing from the pleasure he had given her, he wanted nothing more than to make love to her in the way that people did when they sought to create something permanent.

The thought shocked him. Was he actually thinking…? Was he actually thinking that he wanted to create a baby with her?

At one time that mere thought would terrify him, but this time it settled over him like a blanket of warmth.

She reached for him. "Baby…"

"I won't keep you waiting. I promise."

The condom on, he went onto the bed beside her. As his lips sought hers, he wanted to tell her that he loved her. It was an overpowering urge, yet he didn't want to scare her.

Damn, he was scared himself.

She reached for his shaft. "I need you."

Marshall wasted no time settling between her thighs. As

he kissed her, he filled her. And she cried out. That feathery, soft cry.

It was a moan of pleasure that reached deep inside of him and settled in his heart.

Chapter 19

The next morning, Tamara and Marshall were on the way to Toronto when her cell phone rang. It was early, barely eight, which alarmed her. Quickly digging her phone out of her purse, she saw Callie's number—which concerned her even more.

Praying that everything was okay with Michael, she answered the phone. "Hello?"

"Hey, Tamara. Sorry to call you on your weekend away. And I know it's early, but—"

"What is it?" Tamara asked, picking up on the urgency in Callie's tone.

"It's the shop," Callie said, then sighed. "Look, there's no easy way to tell you this. But sometime during the night, it was vandalized. The front windows are busted. The chairs have been trashed. Lights ripped from the ceiling. The cash register was stolen."

Tamara held her cell phone in her hands, too stunned to speak.

"Tamara? Are you there?"

"I—I'm here."

She saw Marshall look at her from the side of her eye. He asked, "What is it?"

"We—" She could hardly catch her breath. "We have to turn around."

"What?" he asked.

Tamara stifled a sob. "It's Callie. She said…" Her voice trailed off as her stomach clenched painfully.

Marshall took the phone from her hand. Tamara could hear him asking Callie what had happened.

Her salon, her dreams. Why was this happening to her?

"Ask her how bad it is," Tamara suddenly said.

Marshall's forehead was scrunched with worry. "Right. Wow."

"Ask her how bad it is."

"Tamara wants to know how bad it is."

But Tamara didn't wait for Marshall to tell her. She pried the phone from his hands and asked Callie herself.

"Tamara, I wouldn't have called you if it wasn't bad. The place is totally trashed. I'm really, really sorry."

Tamara had been trying to hold in her emotions, but she no longer could. She started to cry.

Marshall took the phone from her. "Tell Nigel to call me in my car," he said. "That way I can talk to him on speakerphone." He then disconnected the call, placing the phone on the console.

Tamara rested her head on the car window, sobbing heavily.

"I'm sorry, Tamara," he said. "God knows, I'm sorry."

She said nothing. Marshall exited the highway and pulled the car into a gas station. Then he unbuckled his seat belt and slipped his arms around her.

"Baby, it'll be okay."

"How?" Tamara demanded. "How can it be okay? My salon is gone. And so are my dreams."

"We'll go home. See how bad it is."

"It's over," Tamara said, feeling numb.

"You've got insurance. Things can be replaced. I'm just glad it happened when no one was there."

Marshall held her for a long while, until her tears stopped. "You sure you don't want to head on to Toronto, take the course you were planning?"

"What's the point?" Tamara asked. She was despondent. Crushed. "Please, take me home."

"Okay," Marshall said. "If you're sure."

Tamara wasn't certain of anything anymore.

Several minutes passed. Marshall kept quiet, clearly realizing that she needed her space.

Tamara was the one to break the silence. "I...I got a note."

"Pardon?" he asked.

"The night of my launch. I got a note. I saw it after everybody left."

Marshall narrowed his eyes. "What did the note say?"

"It was a threat."

His lips parted, and he stared at her with a look of disbelief on his face. "What?"

"I realize that now," Tamara said, her voice void of emotion.

"What do you mean you realize that now? If it was a threat—"

"Someone told me to go back where I came from. That I'd been warned."

"Why didn't you tell me?"

"I figured it was just someone who was upset that I was opening the salon. I never expected..." Her stomach lurched painfully.

"Damn it, Tamara. You get a note like that, and you don't tell me? I'm a detective, for God's sake."

"How could I know it was more than some stupid note?" Tamara snapped.

"No matter how I try to be there for you, you shut me out. Did it ever occur to you that the guy who attacked you and this note may be related? Maybe the same person behind both?"

Tamara shook her head. "Some punk off the street? And a note from an angry business owner? I don't see the connection."

"That's because you're not a cop." Marshall slapped the steering wheel. "At the very least, I could have made sure this was looked into. Heck, I could have arranged for security at the shop while you weren't there."

Tamara's tears threatened again. On top of hearing this awful news, Marshall was furious with her.

She had spent the past year becoming self-sufficient, getting emotionally stronger. She had been on a mission to carve out her own path in the world—independently.

"I hate that you didn't trust me with this," Marshall said, shaking his head.

"It's not about trust," Tamara countered.

"Isn't it?" He gave her a pointed look.

"Think what you want," she told him.

"Obviously, I have to."

Tamara wasn't sure how much time had passed, but when she saw they were at the U.S. border, she realized that she and Marshall hadn't spoken for more than thirty minutes.

Once they were through the border crossing, Tamara broke the silence.

"I came back to Cleveland for a new start. I thought…" She shook her head. "I was stupid."

Marshall blew out a frazzled breath and then faced her for a moment. "I didn't mean to come down hard on you. But don't let whoever did this win. There are risks with running a business, no matter where you set up shop. There are no guarantees anywhere."

"I know that, thank you," she snapped. "Obviously, there are no guarantees in anything."

As Tamara looked at him, she saw the flash of confusion and disappointment in his eyes as he focused back on the road. She knew she'd hurt him, but she was too hurt herself to even apologize.

Because what was the point? She had been setting herself up for disaster from the beginning.

As they drove back to Cleveland, she fought the feelings of overwhelming despair. Feelings that were all too familiar from her time with Patrick. She had spent a year trying to put her life back together, but now it seemed that it had all been for naught.

The truth was, she knew how it felt to live in fear of losing your life. It was the worst feeling in the world. If someone was out to get her in Cleveland—as well as destroy her livelihood—then what kind of future could she have there? She could rebuild her shop, but then what? For the same utter devastation to return when it was vandalized again? She couldn't bear the possibility.

That was the decision Tamara had come to during the drive home, and when she returned to Cleveland and asked Marshall to drive by her shop, the decision was finalized in her mind.

She went into the utterly destroyed remnants of her once-beautiful salon. As she looked around at the devastation, she fell to her knees and cried.

"I'm sorry," Marshall said as he went onto his haunches beside her. "This is worse than I thought. Worse than I imagined."

He placed an arm on her shoulder, but Tamara shrugged away from his touch.

"The police will do everything to determine who the culprit was. Bring him or her—or them—to justice."

"Yeah, I'm sure. They'll be real successful, won't they? I didn't even get my security cameras installed yet. That was supposed to happen this week."

"I know how you must feel. But you can rebuild."

"How?" she demanded, looking at him. "How can you know how I feel?"

"I'm just saying—"

"There's nothing to rebuild here. It's over. I'm going back to Florida."

Tamara shot to her feet. Marshall narrowed his eyes as he looked at her. "You—you're what?"

"There's no future for me here. I don't belong here. People

don't want me here. I was stupid to believe I could make my
dreams come true in Cleveland. I'll go back to Florida, back
to the resort where I sold time-shares. No one can take that
from me."

"Wow." Marshall's jaw flinched, and an inexplicable emotion passed in his eyes. "Well, if you feel that's what you need
to do, then that's what you're gonna do."

As Marshall turned and walked out of her destroyed salon,
Tamara felt fresh tears sting her eyes. Because in that moment,
she realized she had lost more than the salon.

She knew she'd told him she was leaving, but he hadn't
asked her to stay. Which, as hard as it was, was probably for
the best. Because she had her son to think of. And she wasn't
about to stay in Cleveland where some idiot might try to attack her again, and possibly leave her son without a mother.

She would return to Florida. It was the only option left.

Even if she left Cleveland with a broken heart.

Marshall dropped Tamara at Nigel's house and didn't bother
to go inside. He would talk to Nigel later and gather the details
about the vandalism. But now he needed to be alone.

He went into his house and slammed the door behind him.
He had an urge to grab something, smash it. Anything. He
wanted to do something to assuage his pain.

But breaking something wasn't going to help.

Nothing would. Tamara had just cut him out of her life as
if he didn't matter to her one bit.

Yesterday, she'd been in his arms, responding to him with
a ferocity that turned him on like nothing before ever had.
Today, she told him she was heading back to Florida, their relationship be damned.

He'd wanted to tell her not to go. To tell her to stay here, assure her that he would always protect her. But one thing he'd
learned about Tamara—you couldn't make her do what she
didn't want to do.

He had gone at the pace she'd wanted, tried to prove to her

that he cared for her. But along the way, he hadn't truly taken the time to examine his own feelings. It wasn't until yesterday that he'd realized he wanted her in his life forever.

He loved her.

And now she was leaving.

Just like Lisa had left him.

Only this time, Marshall was far more devastated.

He hadn't thought it possible, but he had fallen for Tamara more deeply than any woman he had loved before. He'd loved her spunk and her fire. He'd admired her fight and her resolve.

But the same things he loved about her were also going to cost him the woman he loved. Tamara, a newer, stronger person since her divorce from Patrick, clearly wasn't going to let any man stand in the way of any decision she wanted to make.

Sure, he could plead with her to stay, but what was the point? While he had been falling for her, she had still been keeping him at arm's length. For God's sake, she hadn't even told him about the threatening note she'd received. It wasn't as if she didn't have the time during their four-hour drive from Cleveland to Niagara Falls. Yet, she hadn't confided in him—*and* he was a police officer.

That told him that despite their sexual relationship, she didn't trust him. The only time she gave him all of herself was when they were making love.

If she were any other woman, her feelings would have started to build. But she was one determined not to let a man hold her down again, so she had been able to keep her walls up, even when it had appeared to Marshall that she was letting them down.

Marshall remembered all too well their earlier conversation about her pursuing a career as a hairstylist. She'd made it clear that Patrick hadn't approved, and how she'd had to sacrifice her true passion because he hadn't believed in her dreams. The last thing that Marshall wanted to do was ask her to give up her new goals for him. If she stayed in Cleveland and things didn't work out, she would be bitter.

The greatest hurdle to them having a future together was the fact that she likely would never truly trust another man again.

Sadly, Marshall had to acknowledge that there was nothing he could do about that.

Chapter 20

"Why?" Michael demanded, rising to his feet.

Tamara looked at her son. She had just explained to him that they would be heading back to Florida in a couple of days.

"Michael, sit down."

"No! I don't want to sit down. You're ruining my life!"

Tamara took a step toward her son, but he took a step backward. His eyes were enlarged, and he was on the verge of tears. She had known he would be upset by the news of their departure. But he was her son, and he had to do what she wanted to do. It was best for them that they leave. She couldn't risk getting hurt or killed at the hands of some crazed person with an agenda. She had to protect herself and Michael, at any cost.

They stood in her bedroom at Callie and Nigel's house. "Michael, my shop was vandalized. Someone already attacked me—you know that. What if I fix the shop and it happens again? What if I'm there when someone comes back to do more damage?" She stepped toward him. "I can't risk you or me getting hurt, honey. I thought we could make a life here. That's what I wanted. But things have happened to change my views. I know you're happy here, and I'm sorry. But you were happy in Florida, too. You can be happy there again."

"But I don't want to move back there."

"I know you're going to miss Kwame. Living here, you two have been like brothers. But we'll come back and visit. I promise."

"No!" He shouted the word.

"Michael," Tamara began firmly, "you watch your tone with me. I'm your mother, and I know that this might not sound like a good idea to you, but I'm the one who still has to make the decisions for our family. You're only eight years old."

"It's like you hate me or something!" Then his tears came, big tears rolling down his puffy cheeks.

Tamara stepped toward him and wrapped her arms around him. She hugged him to her chest while trying to hold back her own tears. "Of course I don't hate you." He didn't realize that it was hurting her to leave, too. "Everything I do, I'm thinking of your best interest."

"Moving back to Florida isn't in my best interest," Michael countered.

"I know you like it here, and—"

"I want to stay here. We could stay with Marshall. I want him to be my dad. He would keep us safe. Why do you want to take me away from him?"

Tamara's heart ached. Even as she'd gotten involved with Marshall, the one thing she'd wanted above all else was to protect her son. That was why she'd kept her relationship secret, and no strings, because she didn't want her son getting emotionally involved with a man she wasn't sure would be in her future.

Despite that, Michael had fallen in love with Marshall anyway. And by leaving, he was going to feel as though he had lost a second father.

"Sweetheart, I'm sorry. I really am. I know you get along well with Marshall."

"I love him."

"He's a great guy. He's been a great influence in your life. I know that. But—"

"He loves you, but you don't love him."

Tamara's heart fluttered. Lord knew, she hadn't wanted to examine her feelings, because the last thing she wanted was to fall in love. But against the odds, she *had* fallen for him. She had fallen for the man she had once deemed a playboy.

That scared her. If she truly gave her heart to Marshall, she would be opening herself up to be hurt.

And that was something, at least right now, that she couldn't handle.

At the end of the day, she didn't really know how he felt about her. But she knew she had to take the blame for keeping him at arm's length. She had come out of a disastrous marriage, and she didn't want to allow herself to be vulnerable.

Now you're running away...

The words sounded in her head, as if someone else had spoken them.

Tamara swallowed, uncomfortable with the thought that she was fleeing. "Sweetheart, I'm so sorry. You just have to trust me."

Michael sobbed against her shoulder. She had known he wouldn't be happy, but she hadn't expected him to take it this hard.

"I just want a real family," he sobbed.

"You *have* a real family," she tried to assure him, gripping his shoulders and looking into his eyes. "We are a family."

Michael shrugged out of her touch and ran out of the bedroom. Tamara debated going after him but decided that for now she would let him be. He was upset, and she couldn't blame him. But he was too young to understand the dynamics of the situation. With this second attack on her salon, she no longer felt safe. And if she didn't feel safe, the same smothering feeling of terror would haunt her.

Tamara couldn't deal with that again.

Eventually, Michael would get over this. He was a tough kid.

Stressed and upset, Tamara lay on the bed and drifted off to sleep. She didn't wake until a couple of hours later.

Heading out of the bedroom, she went in search of Michael to see how he was coping. She also wanted to take him and Kwame to a movie, something to lift his spirits.

Maybe even dinner at his favorite pancake house. He loved to have pancakes for dinner. She would try to give him whatever he wanted.

"Hey," Callie said when Tamara wandered into the living room. "How are you feeling?"

"Well. Not good. But what can I do?"

"You can stay with us and not worry about the salon. I'm sure whoever did it will be caught, and then you can rest easy."

Hugging her chest, Tamara nodded. She knew that Callie meant well, and maybe she would feel differently tomorrow, but as of right now, Tamara needed to get out of here. Call it running, but for her sanity, she felt the need to get away.

"Where's Michael?" Tamara asked. "Is he in the backyard with Kwame?"

Callie gave her an odd look. "I thought he was in the bedroom with you."

Tamara's face dropped. "What are you talking about?"

"Michael was in the bedroom with you." Callie sounded confused.

"No." Tamara started to feel panic. "We were talking, and he was upset. Then he left the bedroom." Her brain was scrambling to make sense of what Callie was saying. "You haven't seen him?"

Callie began to rise from the sofa, where she had been sitting reading the paper. "He's got to be here somewhere."

Tamara hurried to the patio door. Sliding it open, she looked outside. Nigel was out there, working on the shed that he had been building. Kwame was by his side.

Callie moved beside her as she stepped onto the deck. "Hon," she called out to Nigel. "Have you seen Michael?"

"I thought he was in the house," Nigel replied.

Hearing Nigel's reply, Tamara whimpered. She quickly ran back into the house, where she looked through every bedroom and closet. Michael was nowhere inside, at least not upstairs. She ran down to the basement and looked everywhere. The laundry room, behind the furnace, in the home theater. Behind boxes.

She saw him nowhere.

Spinning around, she all but bumped into Callie. "I don't see him," Callie told her.

It wasn't possible. He had to be here somewhere. Tamara charged up the stairs and ran to the front door. He wasn't on the porch. She went down to the end of the driveway and looked down both ends of the street.

Again, no Michael.

"No!" she cried. "How can he just be gone?"

"Nigel is calling the police," Callie explained. "Then he's going to start canvassing the neighborhood. We all are. I'm so sorry. We thought he was in the room with you. There was one time when Kwame and Nigel and I were in the back. That must've been when Michael slipped out the front. Do you think he tried to go to the park or something and got lost?"

"He was upset with me. I told him we were heading back to Florida soon, and he wasn't happy about it." Her stomach tightened painfully, causing her to double over. But a few moments later, Tamara stood tall. Her son was out there somewhere. And he needed her. "I'm going to check the park."

"I'm coming with you," Callie said.

Together, they ran a few blocks over to where the park was. Michael knew better than to go to the park on his own, but he had been upset.

But when they got to the park, amid the other kids there and the teenagers, there was no sign of Michael.

Tamara ran to the nearest woman, one who was guiding her toddler up the steps to the slide. "Excuse me?" she began urgently. "Have you seen a little boy out here? He's eight years old. He's about four foot four." She tried to give a more detailed description, thinking that she had been foolish not to bring her cell phone in order to be able to show people a picture.

But she had fully expected to find Michael at the park.

The woman gave her a look of concern. "No," she said. "I'm sorry. I haven't seen anyone like that."

Frantically, Tamara asked everyone there if they had seen her son. No one had.

"He's got to be nearby," Callie said reassuringly. "He couldn't have gotten far. Let's start going through the neighborhood, street by street."

That was what they did for the next hour and a half, knocking on doors, asking people on the street if they had seen Michael. Calling out to him.

No luck. He was nowhere.

That was when Tamara's brain went into overdrive, her fears taking control. Had he been abducted? While not likely, it certainly wasn't impossible. A boy wandering the neighborhood, unhappy, alone... He would have been easy prey for a predator.

"Callie, where could he be?" she asked, terrified.

"He's somewhere. I know he is okay. We're going to find him."

Tamara knew all too well that fairy-tale endings didn't always happen in real life. She knew that bad things happened to good people all the time.

"But what if we don't?" She burst out into tears. Callie drew her into an embrace and gave her the only support she could at that moment.

Tamara was devastated. Her son was gone. The sinking feeling in her gut told her he had run away.

All because he hadn't wanted to go back to Florida.

She'd been trying to make the right decision, but maybe she'd made the worst decision of all.

Chapter 21

Marshall had just finished saying goodbye to his friend Steve, who'd brought his dog, Sherlock, over because his wife had gone into labor, when he got a frantic call from Nigel. "What?" Marshall asked, his stomach sinking. "You're saying Michael *ran away?*"

"It seems so," Nigel said. "Tamara said that she told him they were going to be moving back to Florida, and he got very upset. He left the house without any of us knowing. We've been looking through the neighborhood. The police are here. They're going door-to-door. The neighbors are out here, as well, trying to help. But so far, there's no sign of him in the neighborhood at all."

Good God, this couldn't be true. Marshall's head was throbbing, and he didn't know how to process this news. With the extensive search going on for Michael, shouldn't he have been found already? What could've happened to him?

"Where's Tamara?" Once again, why hadn't she called him? But he digressed. He could imagine she was out of her mind with worry.

"She's back in the house. We had to force her in here. She's hysterical."

"I'm on my way."

Marshall ran out of his house, Sherlock bounding outside with him. "All right, buddy," he said, then opened the passenger door for the dog. "You can come with me. You can help me look for Michael."

Once behind the wheel, he drove to Nigel's house as quickly as he could. Fear seized him. Michael was only eight years old. If he hadn't been found already, where on earth could he be?

"He's somewhere," he told himself, determined to stay upbeat. "He's somewhere safe, probably just scared. He's going to be just fine."

He didn't want to allow himself to think the worst. He would be strong for Tamara.

Even if in his heart, he was scared beyond measure.

When Marshall got to the house, he greeted the many officers he knew and then went right inside to find Tamara. He found her on the sofa, her knees pulled to her chest, sobbing. Callie was beside her, offering comfort.

"Tamara," Marshall said softly. She looked up at him. Her eyes were red-rimmed and swollen. She got up from the sofa and threw herself into his arms. He held her as she cried, and it felt good to be there for her, to be the rock that she needed. He would see her through this. They would find her son.

"Marshall, it's my fault," Tamara sobbed. "I told him we were heading back to Florida, and he didn't want to go. I didn't listen to him. I told him that I knew what was best. And now he's gone."

"No, don't blame yourself. It's not your fault. I'm sure he just went out in the neighborhood and somehow got lost."

"I want to believe that. But I know that he's run off. Why did I push him? Why did I threaten to take away the only security he has right now? He's been through so much in the past year."

"Stop," Marshall told her softly. "You're an awesome mother.

Do you know how much I admire you? Michael knows that you love him. He may not have liked that decision, but you can't blame yourself for planning to do what was best."

"But it wasn't best," she said. "I see that now. He didn't want to lose you, which was going to happen if we left."

"He said that?"

"Yes," Tamara said, barely able to speak through her tears.

"Don't beat yourself up, Tamara. Please."

"You don't understand. I put him in a situation where he felt as if he was losing everything. Yes, I wanted to leave because what happened at the salon had me terrified. All I could think about was running. But it wasn't just the salon I was running from…." Her face contorted in pain. "I was running from opening myself up to you. I'm so scared of being hurt again."

Despite the gravity of the situation, her words filled Marshall's heart with warmth. He drew her close and smoothed his hand over her hair. She cared about him, more than she had wanted to let on. And Michael cared about him, too.

"He couldn't have gotten far. We'll find him." When she sobbed, he tilted her chin upward and made her look into his eyes. "I *will* find him."

It was a promise—one Marshall intended to keep.

"Why has no one found him yet?" she asked in a feeble voice. "Marshall, what if he was picked up by…by someone who will hurt him?"

"Have you called all of his friends?" Marshall asked.

Tamara nodded. "Yes. I called everyone I know, every place I could think of that he might go to. I've let the mothers of his new friends in the neighborhood know to be on the lookout for him."

"Which is all very good," Marshall assured her.

Her face crumpled, and she began to cry. "How can it be good? I don't understand why no one has found him. How hard can it be to find a little boy in Cleveland in broad daylight?"

"I hate to see you in pain," Marshall said. "All I've ever wanted to do since I met you is take away the pain I saw in your eyes. The sadness. Finally when it was gone, you don't know how happy that made me. I promise you I will make sure your son gets home, if that's the last thing I do."

Tamara clung to him, gripped his shoulders as deep, chest-heaving sobs rocked her to her core. It broke Marshall's heart. He felt helpless, and it wasn't a feeling he liked. Michael needed to be with his mother.

"I don't want to leave you, but I have to do my part to help. Call me if you need anything, at any moment."

Callie, whose eyes were also red from crying, came to stand beside Tamara. "I'll be with her. Marshall, you go on. I think that you and the rest of the police force and others looking for him is adequate. You don't need me. Tamara needs me." She slipped an arm around Tamara's shoulders. "The moment you know anything, call us."

Marshall hurried out the door. He got into his car and headed to the basketball court that he had taken Michael to on more than one occasion, but a quick glance around told him that the boy wasn't there. Still, he got out of the car and did a more detailed search, leaving Sherlock waiting in the car. He looked under playground structures where the child might be hiding. He didn't see him. He got back into his car and began driving around again.

He called Nigel as he slowly drove through the streets, which were populated with people who appeared to be out and trying to help.

"We've got this neighborhood covered for several blocks," Nigel told him.

"Then I'm going to head farther east," Marshall explained.

He knew that by now all local police departments would be aware of Michael's disappearance and issuing an Amber Alert. He prayed that someone, somewhere, was paying attention to a little boy lost and contacted the authorities.

Marshall's chest was pained, knowing that the boy didn't want to leave. That in large part, he didn't want to leave Cleveland because of the connection he'd made with him. Marshall's own connection to Michael had deepened since meeting him. He had been falling in love not just with Tamara, but with her son, as well.

When he had met Tamara at Deanna's wedding reception, he had no clue what the future held for him. When they had initially flirted, yes, he had thought about her sexually. Not about a future, but about satisfying a need. Even as their relationship progressed, he had told himself to guard his heart. Tamara wasn't the only one afraid of getting hurt. The times that Marshall's heart had been broken had ripped him raw. It wasn't a pleasant feeling, and it certainly wasn't one that he was anxious to feel again.

Though it was one thing to tell yourself to guard your heart, and another thing altogether to actually be able to do it. Somewhere along the way, he had known that he wanted Tamara in his life for the long term. But he hadn't wanted to voice that sentiment even to himself, for fear of sending her running.

Now, with Michael's safety at stake, there were no more pretenses. If anything happened to Michael, he didn't know how he would deal with it.

Which only drove home the point of how much worse this must be for Tamara. Tamara, who had done her best to protect her son from an abusive husband, was no doubt beating herself up for unwittingly putting him at risk.

Marshall wasn't sure why, but after slowly driving up streets and alleyways for a solid hour, an idea came to him. Though he was certain that Michael didn't even know where he lived, the voice inside of him telling him to head to his house was overpowering.

He had spoken to Nigel only minutes earlier and learned that there were many leads coming in to various police stations, but that so far none of them had panned out. With each minute that passed, much less each hour, he imagined Tamara had to be absolutely devastated.

Marshall had been devastated, too. He didn't want to believe that he would never again see the young boy he had grown to love.

But the idea of checking his house had given him a renewed sense of hope. As improbable as it even seemed that Michael would be able to get there, Marshall knew that even the improbable wasn't impossible. Years of police work had taught him that.

Kids were resourceful. Who knew if he hadn't gotten into Nigel's smartphone and found the contact information that included his home address?

It was unlikely, but not impossible.

At his house, Marshall jumped out of the car. Sherlock leaped out after him, running with him to the front doors. Marshall had locked the house before he left but tried the door just to be sure.

Yep, it was locked.

Marshall then headed along the side of his house, calling out Michael's name as he did. Sherlock, thinking that his looking behind shrubs and bushes was some sort of game, sniffed happily beside him.

"Michael!" Marshall called out when he got to the back of his property. His eyes scanned the backyard, the deck. He trotted down the grass, looking behind tree trunks, much to Sherlock's delight.

Finally, he stood and looked at the back of his house. There was really nowhere else for Michael to be.

Except the Jacuzzi.

Marshall raced for it, opening the covering on the off chance that Michael would have found himself inside there.

Relief washed over him when he didn't see the boy inside. But immediately after the relief came the sense of defeat.

Sherlock, who'd found something of interest in the grass, paid Marshall no mind as he returned to the front of his house. Crushed, he passed the dog to open the door and head inside.

Hours had slipped away, and soon it would be dark. Then the

search for Michael would become even more desperate. As a cop, Marshall knew that every moment that passed was critical.

He would regroup, talk to Nigel and get a sense of what was happening. It was imperative that they found Michael tonight.

Marshall wandered into his kitchen, wanting to grab a quick drink of juice before calling Nigel. Through the patio doors, he spied the dog. He was near the deck now, below the railing to the side.

Perhaps a squirrel had gotten its attention, because Sherlock started barking incessantly.

Marshall opened the back door. "Sherlock," he called. "Come here, boy."

But the dog was too obsessed with whatever had gotten its attention to pay Marshall any mind.

"Sherlock," Marshall called again, stepping onto the deck now. As he approached the railing, he could see the dog pawing at the ground where the deck's framing reached the ground.

"Sherlock!"

Sherlock whined in protest, refusing to give up whatever it was that had gotten his attention.

Marshall hurried down the steps and over to the dog.

"Sherlock, what is it, boy?"

Sherlock began to paw at the framing again, and a fluttery sensation filled Marshall's stomach. He eyed the spot that held Sherlock's interest. The crisscrossing lattice that had been installed beneath the deck to keep critters like raccoons out was ajar at the edge beside the steps, as if it had been pried open—

Marshall dropped to his haunches and quickly looked beneath the deck. And there he was, huddled in the fetal position.

"Michael!" Marshall yelled. Overwhelming relief washed over him in waves. It bubbled from him in the form of laughter. "Oh, Michael—thank God!"

The boy looked up at him with eyes full of tears. There was unmistakable fear on his face.

Marshall pulled back the lattice and reached behind it for Michael's hand. "Come on, Michael. You can come out now."

Slowly, Michael took his hand. It was trembling as Marshall helped pull him out from beneath the deck.

"What are you doing here, buddy? Do you know how worried everyone is?"

"I didn't want to go back to Florida," Michael said, sounding small and frail. "I came here, then you weren't here, and then I realized everyone would be mad at me. So I hid."

"Is that why you didn't come to me when you heard me calling your name?" Marshall asked.

Michael nodded. "I thought you were going to be really mad at me."

"No. Never." Marshall pulled the boy into an embrace. He held him tightly, not wanting to let him go. "Oh, thank God!" He eased back only to wipe at Michael's tears. "Michael, you have no clue how happy I am to see you."

"You're not mad at me?"

"No, buddy. I'm not mad. I love you too much to be mad at you." He smiled, not bothering to brush away the tears that filled his own eyes.

"You love me?" Michael's lips quivered, but formed a grin.

"Of course I love you." He paused. "And you know who else loves you? Your mother. And right now she's scared out of her mind. We have to call her and let her know that you're safe."

Michael's eyes widened with concern. It was clear that the idea was unsettling to him. He had made a decision and now feared the repercussions.

"Your mom loves you very much. No matter what happens, you know that, don't you?"

Michael nodded jerkily.

"Trust me, she loves you enough to understand that you were upset. All that's going to matter to her now is that you're okay. I'm gonna call her and then take you back to the house so you can see her. Everyone's gonna be relieved. Because Kwame, Nigel, Callie—they all love you, too."

He hugged Michael again. And when Michael wrapped his arms around Marshall's neck, Marshall suddenly understood what it felt like to be a parent. To carry the responsibility for a child on your shoulders. He couldn't imagine not seeing Michael again.

His chest tightened with the very thought that this situation could've turned out another way, and he couldn't allow his thoughts to even go there.

Somewhere along the way, this little boy had gotten under his skin and into his heart.

"Let's call your mom, okay? Let her know that you're safe."

Chapter 22

Tamara was running out of the house and toward the car even before it pulled fully into the driveway. Her hands were covering her lips, but her eyes said it all. Her relief was palpable.

She was throwing open the car door as the vehicle was being parked, unable to wait even a moment longer. Michael barely had the seat belt off before she reached in and scooped him out and pulled him into her arms, crying as she held him tightly.

"Oh, my baby! Oh, Michael!" Tears streamed down her face. "Thank God!"

Tamara sobbed as she held him, and Marshall heard Michael crying, too. He had to dab at his own eyes as emotion choked his throat. This was the kind of outcome every cop hoped for in a situation like this.

But he was more than a cop in this situation, more than a person following the case on the news.

He was almost as emotionally invested as Tamara.

Michael said that he didn't want to go back to Florida, that he wanted to stay here and be with him. Marshall wanted the same thing.

"You had me so worried, sweetie. I thought I might never see you again!"

"I'm sorry, Mom." Michael's hands tightened around his mother's neck. "I didn't mean to scare you."

Marshall got out of the car and gazed at Tamara, who seemed reluctant to let go of her son. Finally, she made eye contact with him across the hood of the car. "Thank you."

"Actually," Marshall began, "you can thank Sherlock. He's the one who alerted me to the fact that Michael was outside. I called him, and he never answered me. He was scared he was going to get into trouble. But Sherlock realized that Michael was hiding under the deck."

A look of awe came over Tamara's face. She peered into the backseat where the dog was. She actually smiled.

"Here I was, not a fan of dogs. Now I love them. Thank you, Sherlock, for bringing me back my son."

Now that Michael and Tamara had had their moment, Callie came out the door, followed by Kwame. Callie and Kwame put their arms around Tamara and Michael, all of them sharing a group hug.

Not more than two minutes later, Nigel pulled up at the curb. His grin was as bright as the sun as he exited the car and headed over toward Michael and the rest of the group.

As Marshall watched, he remembered Tamara's words about not feeling as though she belonged in Cleveland. That the vandalism at the shop made her feel as if her place wasn't here anymore. But what Marshall saw, with all the love raining down on her and Michael right now, was a woman who was a part of a family here. She wasn't short of people who loved her.

And he was one of them.

Later, when the proverbial dust settled and all was calm again, one thing was obvious to Tamara.

Marshall was missing. And it didn't feel right.

He had told her when he was going to slip out. She had to speak to the police so they could write their report, and so did

Michael. Marshall felt it was better to call it a night, and she had agreed.

Only now, without him here, she missed him. And so did Michael.

So she got her cell and punched in his number. Nerves tickled her stomach as she heard it ring one, twice, three times—

"Hello?" came Marshall's voice. Deep and sexy. A voice that had made her body shiver with delight when he'd whispered in her ear.

"Hey," she said softly. "It's me."

"I know. Everything okay?"

"Everything's fine. It is now, anyway—thanks to you."

"All I can say is that I'm really happy I was able to find him. I can't believe he hitchhiked to my house, but God was watching over him. The right person picked him up."

Tamara nodded, even as a shudder passed through her. She couldn't imagine what might have happened had the wrong person stopped for Michael. And now she didn't have to.

"Um," she began and then hedged. "Do you...? How would you feel if we came over?"

"Now?" he asked.

"If it's not too much trouble. Michael...well, he keeps saying he misses you, so I told him I'd ask if maybe we could have a sleepover?" When Marshall said nothing, she went on. "I think it will be very comforting to Michael. And then...you and I... well, we can get a chance to talk."

"Hey, that's more than fine with me."

"We can watch a movie or something," Tamara suggested. "I think Michael will love it."

"Come on over," Marshall said.

Tamara's stomach fluttered with nerves as she ended the call. When she shared the news with Michael that they would be going for a sleepover at Marshall's, it was as if he'd been told he could have a private trip to the moon.

About half an hour later, Tamara pulled her car into his driveway. It was dark now, and the colonial house looked stately. But once again the thought struck her that the house was far too big for a single man.

A place like that was meant for a family. A husband and a wife and a house full of kids.

Michael, already wearing his pajamas, was bouncing excitedly as they made their way to the door together. Tamara didn't have the heart to tell him to settle down. It was nice to see him so happy.

She rang the doorbell, and it opened moments later. Marshall's eyes went to Michael first, lighting up. "Hey, buddy!"

Michael vaulted himself into Marshall's arms.

Tamara watched the two of them, a smile playing on her lips. How was it that her son had fallen for Marshall, just as she had? He had put his little life at risk trying to make a few big points. The point that he felt at home here. The point that he finally felt he had a normal life here.

Above all, Tamara knew that he was trying to make the point that he wanted her, Marshall and him to be a family.

Tamara had rejected the idea, out of fear. But now, as she saw the true bond between her son and Marshall, she couldn't help wondering what she'd been so afraid of.

Marshall stood tall, holding Michael in his arms. Then he looked at Tamara, flashing her a soft smile.

As Michael's eyes took in the massive living room, he squirmed free of Marshall's hold. "Wow!" he exclaimed. "This is your living room?"

"Uh-huh."

He looked around in wide-eyed wonder. "This is your house?"

"Yep."

Michael ran toward the TV, checking out the consoles on the television stand. "You name it, I've got it," Marshall said.

"I want to play *Wii Sports.* Can we?"

"Whatever you want," Marshall said.

"Mom, will you play with us?"

Tamara nodded. Then she had to take a deep breath to quell

the happy emotions that were overwhelming her. Seeing her son so comfortable with Marshall…was there anything more wonderful for a mother than this?

"Sure," she said. "Anything you want to play."

And play they did. And laugh.

A bit later, Marshall read Michael a story at his insistence, and then, peacefully, he fell asleep.

Marshall leaned over and kissed Michael on the forehead. Then Tamara did the same.

She was the first one to creep out of the bedroom, followed by Marshall. She went downstairs and took a seat on the sofa. He sat beside her, leaving a little space between them.

"What a day," Marshall said.

"He enjoyed you reading him that story," Tamara said, smiling softly. "Thank you."

"It was no problem."

"I mean for everything," Tamara clarified. "The way you tried to give me hope when you saw me in distress earlier. And then the fact that you were the one to find him and bring him back…honestly, it means more than you will ever know."

"It means the world that I'm the one who found him. Because I was able to keep my promise to you."

Tamara didn't want to cry again. She'd shed enough tears for the day. "Well," she began and blew out a huff of air, "you certainly are the hero of the hour."

"That's a hat I'll gladly wear. Just knowing everything ended well, seeing you both happy…that's my reward."

A few beats passed. Tamara was nervous, she realized. Nervous to tell him exactly how she felt. Nervous because she hoped she hadn't pushed him away.

"You're not just the hero of the hour," she began. "You're the hero of my heart."

A look of uncertainty settled over Marshall's face, and she knew that he was skeptical of her words. After telling him that she wanted to head back to Florida, of course he had to be confused.

"I know you think I'm saying that because of today," Tamara said, "but that's not the case. I can only say that today was a big wake-up call. You go through something like this, and you start evaluating what really matters, and quick."

"What are you saying?" Marshall asked.

Tamara inhaled deeply. "You really got into my son's heart," she said. "In the relatively short time you've known him, you've touched his life in such a positive way. Honestly, I think Patrick is all but a distant memory to Michael. Which is bittersweet, in one way. But more so, it's a good thing."

"Michael's a great kid. He's touched my life, too. I'd be lying if I said I wasn't gonna miss him when you guys head back to Florida."

Tamara swallowed and then inhaled another deep breath. "That's what I'm trying to get at. I think…no, I know I was hasty in planning to leave."

"Really?"

Tamara couldn't read his tone. "Marshall, I panicked. Not just because of the vandalism at my salon, but because of Niagara Falls…" When he looked confused, she continued. "I know I kept saying that I wanted a no-strings-attached relationship, that I didn't want a man to derail my plans. I thought that kind of relationship would be easy with you, because I saw you in the role of player. But the more I got to know you, the nicer you were, the more sensitive…well, the more I cared. But I couldn't tell you that. And God knows I didn't *want* to feel anything for you. Then in Niagara Falls…the way we…the way we were together. It just…it felt like more." She stopped, closed her eyes pensively. "I knew I'd fallen for you, and I was suddenly totally afraid, because I knew that you had the power to devastate me if you didn't return my feelings. I was still scared of *what* I was feeling. I was just one big, hot mess," she said and forced a laugh. "At the end of the day, I couldn't even be upset if you wanted to stay away from me. I just never wanted to be vulnerable to a man again, not after Patrick. Am I making any sense?"

"I get it." He nodded, but again, Tamara couldn't read his tone. "I mean, I get that it isn't easy. Which is why I didn't want to scare you by telling you my feelings were beyond what you were ready to hear. Any decision you were going to make, you had to make it without influence from me. Trust me, I know what it's like to push someone too hard. I've always been haunted by thinking that I pushed Lisa too hard, and that if not for that, she wouldn't have gone back to her ex. And if she hadn't gone back to him, she wouldn't have been…killed."

"No," Tamara said and involuntarily reached for Marshall as she saw the pain in his eyes. She knew this burden was heavy on his heart and wished she could alleviate it. She edged closer to him. "Marshall, what happened to her is not your fault. Trust me, I've been there. I know. She…she just wasn't ready to move past the abuse. I know you feel bad, but you shouldn't hold yourself responsible for that. I understand what she was going through, and I count myself lucky for being able to get away from Patrick. In fact, I know I went from one extreme to the other. I was so determined to be strong and stand on my own two feet, I almost pushed love away." Taking Marshall's hand in hers, she squeezed. "It is *almost*, right? Please tell me I didn't succeed…."

Slowly, his lips curled. There it was, the charming smile she had come to love. "Almost?" he asked. "It wasn't even close. I wasn't going anywhere. Not unless you were going to tell me that you flat out didn't want me. But every time I touched you, I could feel it. I could feel what you couldn't say in words. I was willing to wait. As long as it took."

"Marshall…" His name escaped her lips on a little sob. How was it that she had tried so hard to push this incredible man away?

"And," he went on, "if you'd really decided that you wanted a life without me, I wouldn't stand in your way. If you felt you would be happier without me, I would…" He paused. "Well, love is really about doing what's best for the other person, even if you get hurt in the process."

Tamara's heart filled with warmth and wonder. "Marshall, are you telling me that you would put my well-being above your own?"

"After Lisa and what happened..." He nodded. "Yeah. That's a lesson I learned the hard way."

"Baby," Tamara said, and she slipped her arms around his neck. "Forgive yourself. Don't hold yourself responsible for the decision Lisa made."

"All I knew is that I didn't want to make the same mistake twice. I'd rather be without you, knowing that you were okay, than force you to be with me if it ultimately cost you your happiness."

Tamara's eyes filled with tears, and they spilled onto her cheeks. "Marshall, how could you say that? My biggest fear is that you wouldn't love me the way that I've come to love you."

"Then you've got nothing to worry about," he told her and wiped her tears with the pad of his thumb. "I don't know how you crept into my heart, but I couldn't love you any more than I do. Tamara, you're the one."

"Marshall, I'm not even sure I believe what I'm hearing." Tamara's hands went to her lips, stifling her happy cries.

"Believe it, baby. Life is unpredictable. Sometimes, bad things happen, and it tears you apart. But then, unexpectedly, you're given a gift. Here you came into my life, and you have a son. We get along so well. I love him, Tamara. I love Michael. As much as I tried to be strong for you, when I thought we might not find him...I was heartbroken. Now he's okay, and he's here sleeping in my house. And you're with me. This is one of life's gifts. You'd better believe I'm not going to throw it away."

Tamara grabbed him by the shirt collar and pulled him to her. Then she planted her lips on his and kissed the man she had fallen head over heels for.

"It's exactly that that makes you the hero of my heart. Not what you did for Michael, but what you did for me."

"Baby," he said, his voice raspy. Then he slipped his arms around her waist and gave her a slow, deep, hot kiss that stoked the embers of her desire.

"I love you, Marshall. I really, really do. I'm not afraid anymore. I'm here, and I'm ready."

"And you were worth the wait. I love you, too."

His words were an aphrodisiac. His words thrilled her heart. "I want to make love to you," she whispered.

Marshall's eyes widened in surprise, and then he glanced upward. "But Michael…"

"Will be out cold for several hours." Her lips spread in a smile. "We've got time."

"How much?"

"Oh…enough."

Marshall's eyebrows rose. "Is that right?"

"Mmm-hmm." She gave him a soft kiss on the lips. "Enough time for me to show you just how much I love you."

"That's an offer I can't refuse."

She smiled as they went upstairs hand in hand to Marshall's bedroom.

There they intended to prove with their bodies that they loved each other with all of their hearts.

* * * * *